Paul zeroed in c

coming from.

He pressed an arm against Shelby, keeping her as close to the building as possible and out of the shooter's line of sight.

The front door opened and his dad emerged with a shotgun in his hand. "What's going on?" he shouted to Paul.

"Sniper! Get back inside!"

Paul turned to Shelby. Her face had turned white with fear. No way his brother could say he'd imagined this. "When I say go, we're going to run inside the barn. Okay?"

She nodded but the way her hand clutched his arm told him she was terrified. She had a right to be. But they were pinned down and exposed out in the open. They had no choice but to make a run for the barn. This guy wasn't going anywhere without their intervention. Paul waited for a lull, then pulled Shelby ahead of him.

"Run! Go now!"

Virginia Vaughan is a born-and-raised Mississippi girl. She is blessed to come from a large Southern family, and her fondest memories include listening to stories recounted around the dinner table. She was a lover of books from a young age, devouring tales of romance, danger and love. She soon started writing them herself. You can connect with Virginia through her website, virginiavaughanonline.com, or through the publisher.

Books by Virginia Vaughan

Love Inspired Suspense

Cowboy Lawmen

Texas Twin Abduction
Texas Holiday Hideout
Texas Target Standoff

Covert Operatives

Cold Case Cover-Up
Deadly Christmas Duty
Risky Return
Killer Insight

Visit the Author Profile page
at Harlequin.com for more titles.

TEXAS TARGET STANDOFF

VIRGINIA VAUGHAN

LOVE INSPIRED SUSPENSE
INSPIRATIONAL ROMANCE

LOVE INSPIRED® SUSPENSE
INSPIRATIONAL ROMANCE

ISBN-13: 978-1-335-72231-7

Texas Target Standoff

Copyright © 2021 by Virginia Vaughan

Recycling programs for this product may not exist in your area.

This edition published by arrangement with Harlequin Books S.A.

For questions and comments about the quality of this book, please contact us at CustomerService@Harlequin.com.

Love Inspired
22 Adelaide St. West, 40th Floor
Toronto, Ontario M5H 4E3, Canada
www.Harlequin.com

Printed in U.S.A.

But now, O Lord, thou art our father; we are the clay, and thou our potter; and we all are the work of thy hand.
—Isaiah 64:8

This book is dedicated with lots of love
to the awesome members of the Suspense Squad.
You ladies have shown me friendship, fellowship,
and lots of encouragement and laughter.

ONE

"How are you sleeping?"

Psychologist Dr. Shelby Warren turned to her patient Paul Avery to gauge his reaction to her question.

His left eye twitched as he responded, "Like a baby."

That twitch was his tell that he was being less than truthful. She'd learned to recognize it over the past few days since her week-long evaluation of him began. That was the problem with self-reporting. Even when a patient was trying to be honest—which not all of them were—they still might tell you what they wanted to be the truth.

Paul Avery hadn't convinced her he was ready to return to his duties as a navy SEAL.

"You are staying at your family's ranch while you recuperate, aren't you?"

"Yep, I'm still there, but I'm ready to get

back." He rubbed his left leg, probably remembering the break he'd suffered recently that had set his recovery back. She'd read about it in his file. He'd been hit by an SUV while trying to protect his brother's wife against an attacker.

Typical adrenaline junkie. She saw them all the time. These men thought nothing of placing their lives in danger at the drop of a hat. No matter how she tried to wrap her brain around it, she couldn't understand the instinct to continuously jump into danger. She glanced toward her desk at the newspaper article she'd printed out about a soldier who'd been killed in action. He, too, had been insistent on getting back into combat.

When Michael Finley had come through her office, she'd recommended further counseling for his PTSD symptoms instead of clearing him for duty. Yet her decision had been overridden by her partner, Dr. David Sloan, who had allowed Finley to return to duty. Shelby had been furious when she'd learned about his actions and their horrific consequences. She'd confronted him, but he'd insisted he'd had only Finley's best interests at heart. She wasn't sure whether or not she believed him, but it had gotten her wondering if that was the only time David had interfered with her patients. She was determined to make certain it didn't happen again.

She looked back at Paul Avery. "I received your file from the therapist you've been seeing. He was very thorough, but I have a different way of doing things. I don't rely only on self-reporting of your condition, especially since we have such a limited time for this evaluation. I know you want to go back to your unit, and I know you'll tell me anything that'll make that happen."

He flashed her a curious glance. "You think I'm lying to you?"

"Not lying. No, I wouldn't say your intent is to deceive me. It's more likely you've just convinced yourself that whatever it is that's troubling you is not actually a big deal. But downplaying the problem isn't the same as resolving it. That's why I want to observe you in your home environment and see how you react to stress." She checked her calendar. "We'll finish up the psychological testing tomorrow, then I can be in your hometown—Courtland, isn't it?—next week. Will that be acceptable to you?"

He hesitated, obviously unhappy about this new development, but she wanted him to understand it was nonnegotiable. "I realize this may seem like an unusual step, but it's how I work. I won't sign your evaluation without it."

He sighed, then reluctantly agreed. "Sure, why not, Doc. Whatever it takes."

Whatever it takes. She'd heard that before. But she would make certain another soldier wasn't failed by the process the way Finley had been, even if it meant she could no longer work with David.

"How can you afford to take the time to go to people's homes and watch them? Don't you have other patients who need you here?"

"These evaluations are important to me, so I make the time."

If only her brother Steven's therapist had taken the time, he might still be alive. Shelby remembered when her marine brother had returned stateside, injured and shaken. While his physical wounds had healed, damage had remained under the surface. She had still been in college, but even she could see the signs of PTSD. But he'd insisted he was fine and his doctors had believed him. He'd died six days later, after overreacting to a situation and plunging the rest of his squad into a gunfight.

She stood and turned away from Paul

Avery as thoughts of her brother threatened to overwhelm her. Paul was a navy SEAL instead of a marine, but something about the way he carried himself reminded Shelby a lot of Steven. Ever since losing him, she'd devoted her life to ensuring every military patient she saw received the help they needed.

"Are you okay?" Paul asked. He stood behind her, close enough that if she turned, she would be face-to-face with the handsome SEAL.

It wasn't like her to get so emotional in front of a patient, but that article on Michael Finley had her rattled. She felt like she'd failed him. She'd devoted her life to this mission of helping military personnel, but she wasn't doing enough.

Paul cleared his throat and she felt her face warm. She was going to have a tough time convincing him that she could help him when she was clearly struggling to hold herself together. "I apologize. I shouldn't be getting emotional in front of you."

"That's okay. Everyone has their moments."

She took a deep breath, needing a moment to compose herself before she faced him again. She glanced through the large window toward the tree line across the street, and a shimmer of light in the trees caught her eye. "What is that light?"

She'd hardly gotten the words out when Paul shouted, "Get down!" He tackled her to the floor behind her desk. She didn't have time to even protest before the window shattered. The air was filled with pops of gunfire.

Paul kept his head down and covered Dr. Warren until the gunfire ended. He felt her heartbeat racing and could sense the fear flowing off her. "Are you okay?" After she nodded, he pulled his cell phone from his pocket and leaped to his feet, snapping photos of the tree line the shots had come from. His hand itched for his weapon, but he'd stowed it in his pickup before entering the building.

The ringing of gunfire gave way to frightened screams and bustling all around him as people in the adjacent offices began to emerge from wherever they had ducked for cover. He spotted movement in the trees, and although he doubted he could catch up with the sniper, he leaped through the shattered remains of the window. He might not be able to catch him, but he could make certain he was gone—maybe even see enough to help him identify the shooter to the police. He stopped at his truck to grab his gun.

Going toward the tree line, Paul spotted movement in the bushes and headed toward it, gun drawn. He found a clearing that had to have been the sniper's nest. The sound of a door closing grabbed his attention and he hurried toward it, stumbling upon a man hopping into a black pickup truck. It sped off just as Paul entered the clearing. Still running on his battle-honed instincts, he started to charge after it—but then stopped. He wasn't going to catch up to the guy, not with the way the leg he'd broken six months ago was already stinging him. Who was he kidding? Even when he'd been 100 percent, he hadn't been able to outrun a truck. The sniper was long gone.

But he had something to give the police. He'd seen the truck and the man's back. He could give a brief description of height, build, clothing. It wasn't much, but it was a start.

He turned and stared at the building he'd exited only minutes before. He knelt and held up his arms as if aiming a rifle at the building. This spot was the perfect place for an ambush. He stood and headed back, where a crowd had already gathered in Dr. Warren's office. She was now sitting on the sofa. Two people stood over her, one who he recognized as the receptionist—he thought her name was Colette—and a man he didn't know. Several others were standing at the doorway or by the window, watching. As he approached, he saw cuts on the doctor where the shards of glass had struck her. At least one had hit her forehead, and that wound was bleeding heavily, as head wounds often did. The towel she'd pressed against it was already turning red.

"How is she?" he asked the receptionist.

Colette turned to look at him. "She has a gash on her forehead, but otherwise she seems to be okay. I called 9-1-1."

He nodded and looked around. The doctor was going to be fine, but someone had intended otherwise. He walked over to the back wall and saw several holes where the bullets had gone through to other offices. "Is everyone else okay? Was anyone else struck?"

The unknown man answered. "No, everyone is accounted for. No one was hit. What happened here? Shelby is too shaken up to tell us."

"A sniper shot through this window. I saw him in time to pull her out of the line of fire."

The man's face paled and he took a step backward. "You saw who did this?"

"I saw the flash from the rifle's scope," Paul corrected. "I got a bit more of a glimpse of the shooter when I ran after him, but he got into his truck before I could get a good look at him." It was surprising he'd even seen the truck driving away, since he'd had to stop and retrieve his gun first. A trained sniper should have been much quicker to escape. Why had it taken him so long? And, the more important question, why had he been there in the first place?

"I'm glad you were here and that you have quick reflexes," the man said. He extended his hand. "Dr. David Sloan."

Paul shook his hand. He'd seen the name on the office door when he'd first entered the building. "I'm glad I could help." He trained his eyes on the woman on the couch. "Are you sure you're okay?"

"I'm fine, except for where the glass hit me." The hollow look in her eyes and the way her hands trembled belied her assurances, but he didn't press the matter. She had reason to be shaken up by what had happened.

He was rattled too. He stepped outside and took a long, deep breath to calm the adrenaline racing through his system. The shots had frightened a lot of people, who were now standing around discussing the incident, but he didn't see any signs of damage to any of the other buildings on the block. No bullet holes anywhere else. Those shots hadn't been a random act of terror, meant to scare people and cause a panic.

Those bullets had been meant for Dr. Warren, or at least, for her building.

The police and paramedics arrived and Paul gave his statement. He'd seen the flash of light at the same time Dr. Warren had—but unlike her, he'd known instantly what it was. If he hadn't been there, if he'd been only a second or two later in reacting, Shelby Warren would be dead.

He didn't need a crime scene investigator to tell him what his eyes could see. She'd been standing at the window, and those bullets had come straight toward her.

She'd been the sniper's target.

Shelby's head was aching as she lay in the hospital bed. Her head wound had been stitched up, but her heart was still racing with fear. Who would do such a thing as shoot through her window? The patrol officers who'd arrived at the scene had asked her if she had any enemies, but she couldn't think of one person who would want to harm her. She was nobody, just a simple woman, living a simple and quiet life. Surely it couldn't have been a deliberate act targeting her. It must have been a stray bullet or random deed.

A knock on her door alerted her to a visitor and she sat up on the bed. "Dr. Warren?" the unfamiliar man said as he walked in. "I'm Detective Murphy. I've been assigned to investigate your case. What can you tell me about the incident?"

She took a deep breath and tried to focus her thoughts. She wanted to be as accurate and detailed as possible so they could hopefully capture whoever had taken that shot, but her memory of the events was scrambled. "I was standing by the window looking out at the trees and I saw a flash of something. Paul—the patient who was with me at the time—tackled me just before the window shattered." For some reason she couldn't fathom, the memories of the weight of his arms surrounding her and the strong beat of his heart were sharp and clear.

"He's the one who ran after the shooter?" the detective asked, waiting for her nod of confirmation. Once she gave it, he continued. "I've already gotten his statement. Good thing he was there. This could have ended very differently."

In other words, she could have been killed. That thought was not lost on her. She shuddered at his words and tried to rub chills from her arms. She was thankful Paul had been there and that he'd reacted swiftly and effectively. It seemed that it paid to have a well-trained navy SEAL in your office during an attack.

"Do you have enemies that you know of or anyone who might want to harm you?"

That answer was easy, and it hadn't changed since she'd spoken to the patrolman earlier. "No." She couldn't imagine anyone she knew was violent enough to shoot at her.

Detective Murphy didn't seem convinced. "You're a psychologist, right?"

"That's right. I perform evaluations of military personnel who've been injured or incapacitated, to determine if they're psychologically ready to return to active duty. I also do some counseling on occasion for military and first responders."

"I imagine you've had patients who weren't too happy with your recommendation."

Of course she had. All the men and women she evaluated wanted to get back to work. Everyone wanted to feel useful in their chosen careers. Sometimes she agreed that they were ready. But there were times when she didn't. "Some do get irritated when I won't immediately approve them for active duty, but that's no reason to try to kill me, is it?"

He didn't verbalize that he thought she was naive, but his expression registered it. "Can you give me the names of some of those patients who were unhappiest with you? I can check them out."

A few names came to mind, but she wasn't going to subject them to a police investigation after all they'd already suffered, at least not without more evidence that they were involved.

"I'll have to take a look at my files," she said noncommittally.

"Why don't you let *me* take a look at those files, and we'll sort it out for you."

She shot him a quizzical look. "The contents of those files are confidential, and you know that, Detective. I'll go through them myself and get back to you with any names." After the incident with Michael Finley, she'd already started going back through her files anyway. She'd even asked Colette to pull several for her to review. Only now she would have to make a separate stack for anyone who might be capable of hurting her.

"I spoke with your partner, Dr. David Sloan. He says you evaluate a lot of Special Forces fellas. Men who've seen as much combat as they have can become very violent, Dr. Warren. Plus they're well trained. If you've gotten on the wrong side of one of them, you might not want to underestimate just how dangerous they can be."

He didn't have to tell her. She knew exactly what some of her patients were capable of, but that didn't mean any one of them had chosen to target her. It also didn't mean she was going to open her patient files to him. "You know I can't allow you to search through my files without a warrant, Detective."

He locked eyes with her but she wasn't going to cave. Finally, he nodded and slipped his notebook into his pocket. "I'll await those names from you."

He turned to leave and she saw David standing in the doorway. He waited until the detective had departed before he entered, his face going pale as he saw her. "Shelby, you look much better. What did the doctor say?"

"They say I'm fine. Just some cuts and a few stitches needed."

"Good, good. I brought your purse. I thought you might need your keys, phone, whatnot."

"Thank you." She was glad to have it. It had been thoughtful of him to bring it. They weren't exactly close, but they'd always had a congenial working relationship. She'd joined David's practice five years ago when it had grown beyond what he could handle himself. She handled most of the military evaluations and did some counseling, while he handled bigger issues and, as a psychiatrist, prescribed medication as warranted. It was his passion for helping soldiers with combat-related PTSD that had drawn her to the partnership. She admired him, or at least she had until she'd discovered he'd overruled her recommendation on Michael Finley. Plus he'd been the one to tell that detective about her work and that irritated her. "Why did you tell that detective that one of my patients might be after me?"

"He asked me what kind of evaluations you perform and I told him. Let's face it, Shelby. If one of your patients doesn't like your recommendation, they could get very nasty." She started to protest, but he cut her off. "You lost your brother and I'm sorry about that. I understand you want to help people, but you are evaluating some of the most dangerous men this country has ever produced. And sometimes your recommendation is the only thing keeping them from doing what they love. That's liable to elicit some bitterness on their part."

Anger burned through her at his tone, at the way he almost made it sound like she'd brought this on herself, just because she looked out for the best interests of her patients. She knew he didn't necessarily agree with her recommendations—Michael Finley was proof of that. But she had hoped that he at least respected her work and her choices, most of the time if not always. He was happy to collect the contract money the government paid them for performing this service, without concern for her safety, at least before today.

He reached for her hand. "I'm sorry this happened to you, Shelby."

"David, it wasn't your fault." She gripped his hand and some of her irritation faded.

"I feel responsible. I told Colette to cancel all your appointments for the rest of the week."

And suddenly, her irritation kicked in again. "You shouldn't have done that."

"You need time to rest and recuperate."

"I'm fine, David. It's just a few cuts—no worse than if I'd tripped and fallen. I don't need you coddling me. I want to work."

"You're so stubborn," he said, standing and running a hand over his face. "You're on medical leave as of right now, and that's an order."

She chuckled at his posturing. David had been a military psychiatrist for twelve years before leaving to open his own private practice. He might be used to ordering people around, but that didn't mean she'd accept those orders. "I'm not in the military, remember? You're my partner, not my superior officer."

He turned to look at her, then sighed. "You're right. I'm sorry. I'm acting overbearing again, aren't I? You have every right to make your own decisions, but, Shelby, please take some time. You've just been through a frightening ordeal. Don't jump back into work until you're certain you're ready."

His words made sense. Every day, she counseled patients not to rush back to work before they'd had an opportunity to process their trauma. Work couldn't be everything, and after a traumatic event, it could easily become a crutch. It rarely fixed anything and was a dangerous path to go down.

And even before this, her life had been all work and no play for more years than she cared to admit.

A knock at the door grabbed her attention, and she looked up, her face warming at the sight of Paul Avery standing there, flowers in his grip.

Speaking of men who liked to jump back into their work…

David stuffed his fists into his pockets. "Well, I'll let you get some rest. I'll call to check on you later." He headed for the door where he stopped to speak to Paul. "Thank you again for protecting her. I owe you." He reached out and Paul shook his hand. David waved to her, then walked out.

Paul approached the bed and held out the flowers. "How are you feeling?"

She took the bouquet and smelled it, enjoying the sweet, fresh aroma of the carnations. "A little shaky but okay."

"That's understandable after what happened."

She was grateful he'd been there. That he'd

thought to come to check up on her told her Paul Avery was a compassionate man. She liked that about him. And she was grateful to have the opportunity to talk to him about it all. Most of the event was still a blur to her. Maybe he could give her some answers. "What *did* happen? One minute, I was talking, and the next, you were tackling me, then shooting started."

"No, the shooting started first—then I tackled you. I noticed the flash of the scope in the window."

She thought back. "Yes, so did I." Well, she'd noticed the light. She hadn't realized it was a scope. "The police were asking me if I have any enemies. Should I be asking the same of you? Maybe you were the intended target."

He cocked his head and gave her an I-don't-think-so look. "I wasn't the one standing at the window."

She couldn't argue that point.

"So, you can't think of anyone who might want to harm you?" he asked.

"No, no one. I can't begin to imagine who would do such a thing."

"Well, it was a sniper shot and you do

counsel a lot of military. We should check out that angle first."

Were Paul, David and that Detective Murphy all comparing notes outside her door? She started to mention it, then noticed the hesitation in his eyes. "What is it?"

He rubbed his hand on the back of his neck. "I was just thinking… I had time to go to my car, grab my weapon and chase the shooter down before he drove away. A trained sniper should have been long gone once the bullets stopped flying."

She frowned. "I don't understand. Are you saying he wasn't actually a sniper?" True, he hadn't managed to hit her—but she'd chalked that up to Paul's quick response.

"Maybe. It's also possible he was waiting around to see if he could get another shot at his target."

The matter-of-factness in his voice was chilling but also typical in his field. He was trained to deal with people as targets, without any emotion or personal involvement. She shuddered at the thought that the man who'd shot at her might have been standing around watching, even afterward. "Thanks a lot for that image."

"You should look back through your patient list," he advised. "See if there is anyone who might have a grudge against you of any kind. It wouldn't hurt to have the police check those people out."

He was right. If this was an attack on her, it almost certainly had something to do with her job as a psychologist. Her social life was nearly nonexistent, and the last time she'd gone out on a date had been months ago. She doubted that man would have suddenly developed a violent obsession with her. Her life was too dull and boring to elicit any hatred that strong.

Paul stood to leave but turned back. "Oh, and if you need to reschedule coming to the ranch, I totally understand." He gave her a wink, and she couldn't help grinning at his teasing tone.

The nurse entered before Shelby could assure him that she wasn't going to let this attack place her on the sidelines.

"All right, Dr. Warren," she said with a warm smile. "I've got your discharge papers ready to go."

She was thankful to be leaving, but suddenly, going home alone to an empty apartment made her uneasy. She had no family waiting at home for her, and no roommate.

If her attacker found her again, there would be no one with her but her cat, Ruby.

"Is someone picking you up?" the nurse asked. She was a middle-aged woman who reminded Shelby eerily of her third-grade teacher. She had the odd feeling that if the nurse didn't like her answer, she'd get sent to the principal's office.

"I came by ambulance, so my car is still at my office," she replied meekly. "I'll…call a cab to take me home."

Paul, now standing by the door, intervened. "I'll drive you. I've got my truck downstairs, and I'm already here."

The idea of getting into a strange cab unsettled her. At least she knew Paul wasn't the one who'd been shooting at her. She stared up into the deep blue of his eyes and gave him a nod of thanks. "I'd appreciate that."

"I'll bring the truck around."

The nurse watched him walk out then turned to Shelby. "He seems like a nice young man. Polite. You've got a good one there."

"He's not my boyfriend."

"No? Well, that's your loss. He's cute too."

She wasn't wrong. She'd been intrigued by Paul Avery's stunning good looks from the moment she'd met him. The combination of his athletic build, strong jawline, dark hair and startling blue eyes gave him a movie-star attractiveness. But unlike your typical matinee idol, he was also haunted by something and—maybe it was the psychologist in her—she found that appealing too. "I'm his therapist. I can't get involved with a patient."

"A patient who brings you flowers," the nurse pointed out, raising an eyebrow.

"He was just worried— he was there when I was attacked today." She felt her face warm. He'd tackled her to save her life, not for any funny business, but the memory of his arms around her was still so fresh and vivid. As vivid as the shots that had rung out at the same moment.

The nurse let out a sigh full of skepticism but didn't say anything else as she helped her get ready, then wheeled her downstairs where Paul was waiting in a blue pickup. He got out and walked around to open the passenger door for her, then helped her onto the seat. She was still a bit unsteady on her feet and was grateful for the help. She gave him directions to her apartment complex, and a few minutes later, he pulled into a parking spot and helped her upstairs to her second-floor home.

She dug the key from her purse and hovered it over the lock, anxiety flooding her. Was it possible that someone was inside, waiting?

Paul must have noticed her hesitation, because he took the key from her. "Why don't you let me check out the place first." She started to protest, but he continued, "Seriously, it would make me feel better." He was probably lying to make *her* feel better, but she handed him the key anyway. Having him check the apartment for intruders would make her feel safer.

He unlocked the door, then stepped in. "It's clear," he said after several minutes and she followed him inside, suddenly feeling very ridiculous.

She tossed her purse on the counter, never so glad to see home. The day's events had drained her and she couldn't wait to find comfort in the familiarity of her belongings. "Thank you for your help today, Paul. I appreciate it."

"No problem, Doc. I'm glad I was there."

"Me too."

Intellectually, she knew men like Paul stepped into danger's path every day. She'd never really understood that instinct, but today, she was thankful for it. She didn't even want to think about what might have happened if she'd been alone in her office when the sniper had taken those shots.

A thump sounded from the living room and Shelby jumped. She spun around to see her cat had knocked a book off the table. She flushed, embarrassed that she'd been so easily startled. She knew perfectly well that it was a normal response to what she'd been through, but it made her feel extra vulnerable in front of the handsome SEAL.

His blue eyes probed her face. "Are you going to be all right here by yourself? Is there someone you can call to come stay with you?"

There was no one. Steven had been her only sibling, and her parents had been killed in a car wreck two years ago. She had a few friends—more like acquaintances—she could call if she absolutely needed to, but she wasn't at that point yet.

"I'll be fine," she assured him. "Thanks again for driving me home and, you know, saving my life today."

He gave a you're-welcome grin and turned to walk out, glancing back one last time before he closed the door behind him. When he was gone, she made certain the lock was firmly engaged, then went around her apartment to ensure all the blinds were closed. She checked the balcony door and found it was also secure. She wasn't usually so safety conscious, but after today, the need to check and recheck everything was strong. It was a normal psychological reaction after a trauma. The response wasn't entirely healthy, but knowing that didn't change her need to do it.

Once she was satisfied that everything was locked up, she leaned against the front door and tried to slow her breathing. She would work herself into a frenzy if she wasn't careful.

She heated up a frozen meal for dinner and poured herself a cup of tea before settling onto the couch. Ruby jumped up to join her and curled up on her lap.

Shelby teasingly scolded her for giving her such a fright earlier, then rubbed her ears, thankful for the company she provided.

She sipped her tea and settled into the quiet of her small, cozy apartment. She tried to pretend everything was fine, but she remained nervous and edgy until she went to bed that night and sleep finally pulled her away.

Paul headed back to his hotel. Courtland was only a two-hour drive from Dallas, but since he'd signed up for a week-long evaluation, he'd chosen to get a hotel room instead of driving back and forth each day. He unlocked the door and walked into his small, freshly cleaned hotel room. He tossed his jacket onto the bed but couldn't sit still. He was ramped up, nervous about leaving Dr. Warren alone after today's incident. If he hadn't noticed the flash from the sniper's scope, Shelby Warren would be dead. But something about the shooting gnawed at him. The shots had been precise. Only Paul's action had prevented her from being hit. That meant the sniper was well trained, but the fact that Paul had been able to chase him down still bugged him.

So did the certainty that if this guy, whoever he was, wanted her dead, he would try again.

On a purely practical level, if Dr. Warren was harmed, it would delay his return to active duty. He'd have to start over again with a new therapist before he could be cleared. He didn't like the thought of that. He wanted to get this week of testing over with, get the home visit completed, and get back to active-duty status.

But practicalities aside, he didn't want her

to get hurt. He'd known her for only a couple of days, but he already admired her. She was a strong woman, dedicated and, dare he think it, beautiful. He'd seen the photo of a man on her desk. She hadn't spoken of him, but the fellow's marine uniform told him all he needed to know, especially given the hurt in her eyes after glancing at it. She'd lost someone important to her to the service. He knew a thing or two about that too. His best friend and teammate, Terry Sykes, had died in battle, the same shootout that had sent Paul back to the states with a round through his gut and nerve damage he feared would never go away. Try as he might, Paul hadn't been able to save Terry, and his friend had died in his arms.

Paul pulled out the phone and dialed his brother Colby's number, just for something to do and someone to talk to, but the call went to voice mail. His brother worked for the FBI and was probably out on a case. Paul envied him. Being here alone was driving him crazy. His usual social circle was his team, but they were deployed and he wasn't one to go to bars. He felt like a lion on the prowl. He needed to do something to occupy his mind. He was ready to end this, ready to at least return to Silver Star, his family's ranch, where he could be left alone.

No, wait. Dr. Warren was supposed to go there to observe him in his environment. He wasn't exactly looking forward to it, but he was ready to get it over with, get this evaluation completed and submitted so he could finally be reinstated to active duty. The broken leg he'd gotten over the holidays had slowed him down and he could feel his skills rusting away as each day passed. He'd already been out of the action for too long. If he was away for much longer, his unit wouldn't be able to trust him to be up to snuff when he returned. He wasn't even sure he'd trust himself. His reentry would be hard, it would take a lot of practice and retraining, but he was looking forward to being useful again.

Not that his recovery at Silver Star had been boring. Twice in the past year, he'd had to assist his brothers, first Lawson, then Miles, protect the women they loved from danger. Thankfully, in both instances, everyone but the bad guys had had their happy endings. Paul had ended up with two new sisters-in-law—and also a broken leg, which had stalled his recovery even further. For the past few months, there had been nothing to challenge him or put him in any danger at all.

Not that he was looking for another drug runner or mob boss to liven up his life, but the action, much like the action that had occurred this afternoon at Dr. Warren's office, got his adrenaline pumping, and he liked that sensation. He liked feeling as if he'd just hit fifth gear and was ready to race. Liked being in a position to protect someone, to use his hard-won skills.

He grabbed his jacket and his gun. If someone was going to target Shelby Warren, it wasn't going to be while he was around. He would keep an eye on her apartment to make sure the attacker didn't return to finish his task. He couldn't be there for his team, to watch their backs, but he could give himself this new mission and help keep *someone* safe.

TWO

Shelby slept fitfully and awoke early. She called a cab to take her to the office. David had advised her to take some time off, but her apartment was too quiet and unnerving. Even Ruby was giving her funny looks wondering what she was still doing there. When she arrived at the office, the first thing she noticed was that her office window had been boarded over. David must have taken care of that. Good.

She unlocked the front entrance and found no one else inside. She hadn't been expecting anyone at this early hour, but the empty office was no longer the welcoming place it had once been for her. Now it just seemed downright creepy.

She clicked on the light in her office. Without the light from the window, it was darker in there than she was used to. The glass was gone along with the bloodied towels. The carpets had been vacuumed and the bloodstains cleaned away. Except for the boarded-up window, there was no longer any evidence of yesterday's attack.

She walked to her desk and powered up her laptop. As expected, Colette had cleared her schedule. She was still a little miffed that David had instructed her to do so without Shelby's consent, but she was sure he'd meant well. He was worried about her and she was grateful for that. She'd spent so much of her time focusing on her work that she hadn't found time to make or keep up with many friends. Her work was her life.

However, having her schedule cleared out didn't mean she didn't have anything to do. She still had paperwork to finish up, and this quiet time would give her the opportunity to dig through her files and try to figure out who among her patients might want her dead. It wasn't a task she was looking forward to, but if it would help the police track down her attacker, she would do her best. Plus she could take the time today to finish making arrangements with Paul Avery to observe him at his home in Texas. She picked up her phone and sent him a quick text, asking him if he could meet her at her office around noon. His response was immediate and to the point. He would be there. She wondered if her text had woken him up or if he was already awake at this hour because he was an early riser. Or perhaps he was having trouble sleeping; he'd carefully evaded that question in their sessions so far.

For now, her focus had to be on her patient files. She pulled open her filing cabinet, gathered all her patient files and carried them over to the sofa to sort through them. She started two piles—one for those she knew couldn't possibly be involved in this and one for those who might be possibilities, since they had the necessary skills and resented her choice to recommend further counseling. She'd found three names to give the police when the bell on the front entrance door announced someone opening it. She stopped, file in hand, her heart kicking up a notch at the sudden noise. She took a breath but didn't release it again until she spotted David moving toward her open door.

His expression was grim. "Why am I not surprised to find you here. You should be at home."

She stood, walked to her desk, and sat

down. "I can't deal with being at home with nothing to do but worry. I need to be here working. I know you canceled my appointments, but I have a ton of paperwork to catch up on, plus I have to go through my files for the police."

David approached her desk and slammed shut her laptop. "Stop it, Shelby. I insist you go home and get some rest. You've had a terrible shock and you're not processing it."

"I'm fine, David."

"Really? Because aren't those the words you hate to hear from your patients? You can't see how much this shooting has affected you. Besides, the workers are coming in around noon today to replace the glass in that window. You can't be here for that."

Was he right? Was she repressing her feelings about the shooting in an unhealthy way? She leaned her face into her hands and realized she had to think rationally. She had been through a trauma and she hadn't dealt with it. Instead, she'd tried to block out the terror and anger behind the comforting routine of work and her duties.

"You're right. I need to deal with this."

He sighed and pulled up the chair opposite her. "I'm not saying you need to spend a lot of time on this if you don't need to, but you should take at least a day and process it."

"Okay. I will. I'll leave before the workers arrive to replace the window."

Satisfied he'd gotten through to her, David walked back to his office. Within a half hour, Colette had arrived, and soon after, patients began to enter. David called one into his office and shut the door but not before shooting Shelby a go-home look.

She hadn't made it far in digging through her files by the time eleven o'clock rolled around. Realizing the men would arrive soon to replace the window, she gathered up the folders, keeping a few out to review, then locked the remaining ones inside the cabinet. She couldn't leave them lying around when the workers came. Once that was taken care of, it was time to take David's advice and go home.

She slid the files she'd pulled out into her briefcase, along with her laptop. She might be forced to remain at home, but that didn't mean she couldn't do some work later. She could always access the electronic files Colette scanned in, if she needed to, but she preferred having paper copies to look at too. David's advice was sound, but she enjoyed her work, and she couldn't imagine what she was going to do sitting around her apartment all day, talking to her cat.

Colette knocked on her door, startling her.

"I'm so sorry," the young woman said, her expression contrite. "I didn't mean to frighten you."

"No, I'm fine." She took a deep breath to calm herself but this one small incident only reinforced David's claim that she was still on edge. "What do you need, Colette?"

"David said you were leaving for the day soon, so I wanted to tell you before you go that I made the arrangements for your trip next week to Courtland County. I booked you a room for five days at the Courtland Arms Hotel. I'll send the confirmation to your email."

"Thank you. The Courtland Arms? Sounds like a nice place."

"It looks to be, but honestly, there weren't a lot of choices of hotels. That town is off the beaten path."

Paul had warned her that his family's ranch bordered a small Texas community. "I'm sure it'll be fine."

It probably wouldn't take the five days she'd allotted for the evaluation, but she wanted to be sure she'd given herself enough time to get the full picture of how well Paul functioned and handled stress in everyday situations. Plus she wanted to talk to his family about his sleeping habits, hypervigilance and any other signs of PTSD they might have noticed that he'd failed to mention so far.

"Okay. Have a good day, Dr. Warren."

"Thanks, Colette. You too." Shelby gathered up her belongings and walked outside to her car. She was glad to have everything settled about the trip, even if it wasn't until the following week. She wasn't especially looking forward to it, but she thought it was important to observe her patients in their natural environments in order to gauge how they reacted to pressure. Some people in the psychology community might find her process odd, but she found it helpful for determining the truth behind what her patients claimed during their counseling sessions—either with their original therapist or with her.

She'd started her car and pulled out of the parking lot before remembering she'd told Paul to meet her at her office this afternoon. She glanced at the clock on the dash. She'd told him to be there at noon and it was already eleven forty-five. Colette wouldn't have called to cancel that appointment, since she'd set it up herself earlier and hadn't placed it on her schedule.

While stopped at the red light, she found his number in her cell phone and tapped the keypad, then put the phone on speaker.

He answered on the second ring. "Hello."

"Paul, it's Dr. Warren. Have you left for my office yet?"

"I'm nearly there."

"I'm sorry, but I just discovered they're repairing the window in my office this afternoon. We'll have to reschedule or meet somewhere else." The light turned green and she sped off, the phone safely in its cradle on the dash so she could keep both hands on the wheel.

"Why don't I meet you at the coffee shop in ten minutes?" He named a nice, locally owned coffee shop a few blocks from her office.

She smiled at the eagerness in his tone. It was clear he was anxious not to lose any time in this process of getting medically cleared, and she hated to put him off any longer. And that apartment was awfully empty. "That's fine. I'll—" She approached a sharp bend and tried to turn her car in the direction of the road, but the steering wheel locked. She tried again. Still nothing. She hit the brakes to try to slow through the downhill curve, but they didn't work either.

"Is something wrong?" Paul asked.

"My steering wheel won't turn. And the brakes are dead. I can't stop." Panic filled her as her car went off the road and barreled through the brush. She pumped the brakes again. Nothing. She had no control.

"Shelby, try the emergency brake," he ordered, his voice calm and steady.

She pulled on the emergency brake. "Nothing is happening." She screamed as the car drove over an embankment and landed in the lake. The airbag deployed, knocking her back. Lights danced around her eyes and her vision blurred. She wasn't sure if she was injured or having a panic attack. Whatever the cause, darkness was pulling her down.

She couldn't afford to lose consciousness. She was in the water, and the car was beginning to sink. She had to get out before she drowned.

"What was that?" Paul's voice filled the car from the phone on the dash. In contrast to his earlier calm, his tone was full of urgency now and maybe a hint of fear. "Where are you?"

She struggled to put words together to tell him. "I—I'm in the water. I ran off the road and landed in the lake." She jerked at her seat belt, but it wouldn't give. "I can't get out. I can't get out!"

"Where are you, Shelby?"

"I went off the road at the curve by my office. Instead of turning up and onto the bridge, I drove right into the water. Paul, I'm sinking. And I can't get out." She tried the door, but it wouldn't open, so she manually unlocked it and pushed again. It wouldn't budge. The force of the water was too strong. She pressed the window button, but nothing happened. The car had lost power. Even if she could get loose from the seat belt, she had nowhere to go. She was trapped.

Paul's disembodied voice continued to speak to her. "I'm on the way. Stay on the line with me."

Water began to seep into the car from the seams around the doors and filled the tire wells. This was it. She was going to drown, trapped in the car.

She pulled on the seat belt again, but it locked and wouldn't give. She reached for her purse and briefcase and dumped out their contents looking for something, anything to use to cut herself loose—but nothing she had would work.

Her head was spinning from the force of the airbag, and although she fought to remain alert and awake, the water was pressing down on her and so was the darkness.

Paul slammed on the accelerator and zipped through traffic. Shelby had stopped speaking to him, and he suspected she'd lost consciousness. It wouldn't be long before the phone went out, too, once the water hit it.

He needed to call 9-1-1, but he hated to hang up and lose the only connection he had to her. Finally, he had to risk it. He didn't end the call with her, hoping to come back to it, but dialed the emergency number to alert them to what had happened. When he went back to Shelby's call, the line was still open, but he heard nothing but the whoosh of water filling the car and the distant sounds of traffic.

He flew off the exit ramp and through the light, then made a sharp left as he headed toward the curve near her office. He spotted the car-sized hole in the brush off the side and parked on the shoulder. He jumped from his truck and ran down the embankment toward the car in the lake. Only a portion of the top was still visible. It was nearly engulfed and sinking fast.

He hurried back to his truck and dug through his toolbox for a hammer to break her windows. He ran back down the embankment, kicked off his shoes and pulled off his jacket, then waded into the water.

Thankfully, he was a strong swimmer and well trained in underwater rescue. He was alone instead of with his team, and he didn't have his equipment, but he would make do. He couldn't wait on the authorities. Shelby would not have the time for that.

The water grew deeper as he waded in, and once it reached his waist, he dived in and swam for the car.

Just as he'd feared, he spotted her slumped over the steering wheel. The water was murky and red around her, indicating an injury. Thankfully, her head wasn't yet submerged and it looked like she was still breathing. He yanked the hammer from his belt and smashed it against the glass on the passenger window behind her, not wanting to risk hitting her with the glass. Once it shattered, he crawled inside along with a flood of water that whooshed through and filled the car even faster.

The water was to her neck and steadily rising. The pocket of air available wouldn't be around for long. He reached down and tried to unbuckle her seat belt, but the lock jammed. He always had his grandfather's pocketknife on him, so he pulled it out and quickly cut the straps. But getting her out of the car would be the tricky part. Towing her out was going to require her face to be submerged, and since she was unconscious, she couldn't keep her mouth closed and hold her breath. But it couldn't be helped. Delaying would only make the situation worse. Hopefully, the paramedics had arrived and would be quickly able to revive her.

He grabbed hold of her, then pulled her from her seat and out through the back window. She reacted immediately to breathing in the water. She gasped and began to flail, but Paul didn't stop to help or reassure her. He swam hard and fast and broke through the surface in record time, but she already had water in her lungs. He was still several yards away from the shore, and he needed to reach land before she drowned.

He spotted the rescue team on the bank of

the lake and shouted at them that he had her and to get ready. He towed her behind him, and by the time he reached the shore, she'd stopped struggling and had succumbed to the water. He hoisted her up while two firemen waded in to help carry her out.

Paul crawled onto the bank as the other men began treating Shelby. His muscles were screaming, proof that his injuries had taken their toll on his fitness, despite his attempts to stay in shape. A fireman ran to him and draped a blanket over his shoulder. He tried to coax Paul into letting him check him out, but Paul wasn't moving—he wasn't going anywhere until he knew Shelby was okay.

Shelby lay flat and motionless as the paramedics tried to revive her. She hadn't moved on her own since that moment in the water when she'd stopped struggling, and her color hadn't returned. He'd seen drowning victims more times than he cared to count, but usually they could be revived if they received treatment fast enough. She hadn't been submerged for that long, but he had no idea what her underlying injuries were from the car crashing into the lake. They could be the difference between her surviving or not.

"Is there anyone else in the car?" one officer asked him.

He shook his head and waved the man away, his eyes glued to the petite, still figure on the ground.

"What about in the water?"

"No, she was alone," he barked. They had their jobs, and he understood that, but he had all his focus on Shelby and didn't want to pay attention to anything or anyone else until he knew she was going to be okay. She couldn't die here today.

He couldn't be responsible for failing to save another person.

She jerked and began coughing, and the paramedics turned her on her side to choke out the water. A rush of relief flowed through the group and especially through him. He sat down and put his hands on his head.

Thank You, God, for not taking her.

He was surprised by how easily that praise slipped through his thoughts. He'd been skirting around his relationship with God since Terry had died, knowing He was there but refusing to face Him head-on with his guilt and shame. He knew God's forgiveness was infinite, but he didn't want to be forgiven.

He deserved to carry that burden for a while longer.

He laid back on the ground and closed his eyes as he felt the all-too-familiar drain of his energy that came when a mission was over.

This incident had proven a couple of things to him. First, he wasn't physically ready to rejoin his team. And second—two attacks in as many days' time meant someone seriously wanted Dr. Shelby Warren dead.

The paramedics insisted Shelby go to the hospital to be checked out. Even though she would have preferred to go home, she'd lost consciousness and swallowed water, so she was taking their recommendation. She watched from the back of the ambulance as her car was pulled from the lake by a wrecker. She'd had it serviced last week, so she couldn't imagine a mechanical problem had caused this.

Tears pressed against her eyes, threatening to spill out as terror overwhelmed her. She turned her head away from the view and pulled the blanket she'd been covered in up to her neck, seeking warmth to combat the icy fear that filled her.

At the hospital, doctors and nurses came

and went. They drew blood, listened to her lungs and did a CT scan since she'd hit her head and lost consciousness. And when she was finally returned to a room, a police officer was waiting to take her statement. She recounted the events as best she could remember. The way the steering wheel had locked. Pumping her brakes to no effect. Plunging into the water at a high rate of speed.

She got through the recitation without losing control. The officer's manner told her he felt this was nothing more than an accident. She hoped he was right. She wanted so much to believe this had been the result of only ordinary mechanical failure and was in no way tied to the prior day's shooting.

Once he was gone, she turned over and bit her lip hard, trying to hold back the wave of anguish and rage boiling up inside her. Why was God allowing this to happen to her? Hadn't she lost enough? Now He wanted her life too?

Someone cleared their throat and she quickly wiped away errant tears before turning to see Paul standing near the door. His dark hair was now dry and he'd changed the clothes she'd seen him in on the bank of the lake. One of the paramedics had told her that he'd jumped in and pulled her out of the car.

That was the second time he'd saved her life.

He held out his hands and looked embarrassed. "I'm sorry I don't have any flowers this time." His tone let her know he was teasing. Then his expression darkened. "You okay?"

She nodded but couldn't find her voice. Her throat was burning, but she wanted to thank him.

She finally managed to eke out a few words. "The police seem to think this was probably just an accident." She looked at him, wondering what he thought about that. The answer was plainly written on his stoic face and in his hard stance.

"The officer thought that only because he didn't know about the attack yesterday. He knows now, because I told him."

So much for that lifeline she'd been clinging to. "You think someone messed with my car?"

He locked eyes with her. "Don't you?"

She didn't have the strength left to argue. She didn't want to believe that this was an ongoing attempt to kill her. She lived a quiet life.

She tried to be a good person. This shouldn't be happening to her. But the facts certainly pointed that way.

Shortly after, her doctor entered to tell her that her tests came back showing no permanent damage, only cuts and bruises. The doctor wanted to keep her overnight for observation, but Shelby declined. She wanted to go home. Paul offered to give her a lift again and she accepted without argument. He walked her to the door of her apartment and, once again, insisted upon checking inside before she went in. Once he was certain it was safe, she entered.

He didn't linger and she was thankful for that. "I'll be around if you need me, Dr. Warren."

His simple declaration was so sincere that she felt her face warm. Why did his eyes have to be so blue? But his offer to be there for her gave her some comfort. "You've saved my life twice now, Paul. I think you can call me Shelby."

He nodded. "Then good night, Shelby."

"Good night."

She locked up behind him, then showered and changed before crawling onto her bed and wrapping the covers around her.

She didn't understand why this was happening to her, and her first instinct was to cry out to God, but she didn't. She hadn't spoken to God in years, not since her brother's death.

He'd let that happen. Now He was allowing this. No, God didn't answer her prayers, so there was no point in making them.

She didn't realize she'd fallen asleep until something jerked her awake. She sat up and glanced around the room but didn't see anything out of the ordinary. She looked at the clock. Two a.m. She wasn't sure what she'd heard but figured it was probably Ruby. The cat slept all day, then suddenly came alive at night and loved to make noise around the apartment while Shelby was trying to sleep. On normal days, such behavior irritated her, but today was not a normal day. Today, it scared her, leaving her too rattled to go back to sleep. Her body ached and her head pounded, even though the doctors had ruled out a concussion.

She pushed back the blankets and got up as her stomach grumbled. She'd forgotten to eat and now was being reminded of it. She walked to the kitchen and Ruby followed her. Had she also forgotten to feed her cat? Apparently so, given the way Ruby was carrying on, meowing loudly and excessively.

Shelby opened a can of soup and poured it into a pot on the stove before popping the lid on a can of cat food and placing it into Ruby's bowl. Ruby dug into it with a fervor. The soup heated quickly, and Shelby was just about to pour it into a bowl when Ruby started hissing behind her, her weird, nocturnal behavior taking a new and unexpected turn.

Shelby turned to shush her and saw a mountain of a man standing in the entrance to her kitchen. She screamed as he lunged toward her. She slung the pot at him, covering him with the hot soup. He cried out in pain and she managed to slip past him and run to the door. She unlocked it and raced from the apartment as shots rang out, the sound muffled as if the shooter was using a silencer.

She rushed down the stairs and right into Paul Avery.

He grabbed her arms. "I heard you scream. What's happening?"

"A man—a man is in my apartment. He tried to grab me. When I ran, he tried to shoot me."

He pulled his weapon. "Stay here." He took the stairs two at a time, and suddenly, Shelby realized she didn't want to be alone. She was torn between getting as far away from the apartment as she could and rushing back toward it to remain with Paul for safety. She followed him up but stayed by the door as he entered her home, gun raised, and looked around.

With the door open, Ruby ran out, and Shelby grabbed her up and pressed her face against the cat's fur, letting Ruby's soft purr settle her racing pulse.

Inside, Paul moved toward the balcony door, glanced over the railing, then sprinted back through the apartment. "He went over the balcony," he said as he zipped past her and down the stairs. "Call 9-1-1." He took off and disappeared around the side of the building.

Shelby hurried inside and locked the door, then ran to the balcony and closed and locked that one too, then noticed a broken piece of glass on the door. That was how he'd gotten inside. The breaking glass must have been the noise that had awoken her. The whole time she'd been puttering around in the kitchen, feeding Ruby and warming up her soup, he'd been inside her apartment, watching and waiting for her.

She dialed 9-1-1 on her landline, and within minutes, the police and paramedics arrived.

Moments after they did, Paul reappeared, out of breath, from behind her apartment building. "He got away."

She watched him and realized he'd been there the moment she'd screamed. At two in the morning, he'd likely been sitting in his truck, awake, watching over her from the parking lot. "You didn't leave, did you?"

"I figured if he really wanted to get you, he might try again. Besides, my truck is as comfortable as the beds at the hotel. But I could see the balcony from where I was parked. I didn't have my eyes on it the whole time—I mostly watched the door—but still, I don't know how he got past me. He's good."

Detective Murphy approached them both. "Can either of you give me a description of the suspect?"

She shook her head and stroked Ruby's fur. "It all happened so fast. He was big. That's all I remember."

Paul agreed. "I didn't get a look at his face but he was about six-foot-one, wearing dark clothes. He had dark hair. I do believe it was the same man I saw out by the trees at the office the day before yesterday."

"It looks like he climbed up the balcony and broke the glass in the balcony door," the detective told them. "That was the point of entry."

"Has there been any update on what happened to her car yesterday?"

The detective looked solemn. "I spoke with the tech team a few hours ago. Preliminary results show some kind of remote-control device attached to your vehicle. It was probably used to disable the car's computer on command."

Shelby felt an overwhelming urge to crawl under the ambulance and hide. "Then it wasn't an accident." She didn't bother making her response a question. She saw the answer on both their faces. Much as she'd wanted to deny it, she'd known the truth herself, all along. That had been an attack against her as surely as the man breaking into her apartment was now.

The police gathered their evidence, then departed, leaving Shelby sitting on the step outside her apartment, still holding on to her cat, who was growing more restless with each moment. She didn't want to put Ruby down, because the cat might wander off, but she hesitated at going back upstairs to the apartment that no longer felt safe.

Paul eyed her before taking a seat on the step above her.

"He was inside my home, Paul. He invaded my space."

"I know." He reached for Ruby. "Would you like me to hold her for a while?"

She handed the cat over to him. "Would you put her inside and close the door? I'm not sure I'm ready to go back in there just yet."

"Sure." He walked away, returning a minute later to rejoin her on the steps, his long legs stretched out before her. "I doubt he'll be back tonight. I'll stand watch just in case."

She glanced up at him, surprised at his determination to keep her safe. "Why are you doing this, Paul? Why are you here?"

He leaned forward and touched her arm in a way that felt instantly soothing. "I know what it's like to be scared and alone. If I can do something, then I want to help."

His compassion touched her. "Thank you, but I can't expect you to sleep out here forever. To be honest, I'm not sure I want to stay here myself. I don't know how I'm going to go back to my apartment and try to sleep without seeing that man's face—especially knowing he's still out there."

"Well, you were planning on coming to Courtland anyway. Why not pack a bag and go now? It'll probably help you to get away for a while, plus it'll give the police time to figure out who is behind these attacks against you."

She started to refuse. Clearly, traveling with a patient would stretch the bounds of her professionalism, but she did like the idea of getting out of town while the police searched for her attacker. Plus she had a job to complete, and her schedule was already cleared.

She glanced up at Paul Avery and knew it would be a mistake to get too close to the handsome navy SEAL, but she couldn't help herself. Surely she could maintain her professionalism, even under these circumstances. It might be difficult, but she would find a way.

THREE

Shelby sat in the passenger seat of Paul's pickup. She'd thrown some things into a suitcase, left out food for Ruby, slipped a note under her neighbor's door to look after the cat for the next few days, then hopped into the vehicle. Their first stop was to a superstore—open all night, thankfully—where she purchased a few necessities, including a new cell phone and laptop, both of which she'd lost when her car plunged into the lake. They went to his hotel next, so he could pick up his belongings and check out of his room. They picked up drive-through breakfast and coffee to have in the car on the way to Courtland.

A couple of hours later, they arrived. "This is it," he said, turning the car onto a dirt road through a gate with a sign that read Silver Star Ranch. She saw nothing but open fields and blue sky until they reached a farmhouse.

Horses were loose in the corral close by, and what looked like a newly built barn stood a few hundred yards away.

"The old barn was set on fire a few months ago," he explained as they got out of the truck. "We had to rebuild it."

"Lightning?"

"No, arson. Either the same guy that ran me over with his SUV or someone he paid to do it. My brother Miles and the woman who is now his wife were inside it at the time."

"Oh no, that's horrible!" Shelby exclaimed. "Were they hurt?"

"It was a close call, but we got them out," Paul assured her, "along with the horses."

"That must have been terrifying," Shelby said, shaking her head.

"For the horses?" Paul shrugged. "I guess they were spooked, but my brother Lawson and his wife, Bree, have been working with them, trying to rehabilitate them."

In spite of herself, Shelby laughed. "I meant for your brother and his wife, but I'm glad to hear the horses are getting some treatment too." She knew there had been some danger surrounding the brother and sister-in-law that had resulted in the incident where Paul got run down and broke his leg. She also knew he was living with his family while recovering. She was anxious to meet them all and learn from them firsthand how he was adjusting to the new circumstances of his life.

The front door opened and an older couple approached as Paul pulled his bag from the truck. He motioned her over. "Shelby, these are my parents, John and Diane Avery. Ma, Pa, this is Dr. Shelby Warren. She's here to evaluate me to see if I'm ready to return to my team."

His parents were friendly and welcomed her. Another couple emerged from the barn and walked over, and Paul introduced them too.

"This is my little brother, Lawson, and his wife, Bree." He turned to them and introduced her.

Lawson tipped his cowboy hat and said, "Welcome," while Bree reached to shake her hand.

"It's nice to meet you."

"Thank you all for allowing me to come here. I know it's unusual, but I like to be thorough before approving someone to go back to active duty."

"No problem at all," Diane stated. "I'll

show you to the spare bedroom, where you can stay."

"I couldn't put you out. I made reservations at a local hotel." She'd phoned Courtland Arms during the drive to move up the dates of her stay, and they were able to accommodate her early.

"There's no reason for that. We have plenty of room. Besides, it'll be easier for you to observe him if you're here at the ranch."

But it would also place her unprofessionally close to the handsome navy SEAL. She was already closer and probably more emotionally involved with this man than she should be, thanks to how he'd saved her life. Three times. She'd retrieved at least a little of her common sense on the drive today. While it was right and acceptable to be appreciative of what he'd done for her, she couldn't allow that connection to color her judgment of his ability to return to his duties.

And accepting favors from this family, even something as simple as room and board, could be misconstrued. "Thank you, but I think it's best I stay in town for now." She walked around the car, and Paul handed her the keys. Borrowing his truck made her feel guilty, but it was only until she got a rental car in town.

Lawson stepped forward. "Are you sure it's safe for her?" he asked his brother.

Shelby felt her face warm with embarrassment at the realization that Paul had told his family about the attacks against her. It was silly to feel self-conscious about her problems, yet she did. She'd been hoping to leave those behind in Dallas.

But Paul took his question in stride. "We have no reason to believe her attacker followed her here. I made sure we weren't tailed, and no one outside her office, her neighbor and the detective in charge of her case knew she was leaving town."

"I'll be fine," she said with more bravado than she felt. She was still a little shaken over the ordeal, but she agreed with Paul's assessment. She'd gotten out of Dallas to escape her attacker, and they'd taken precautions to cover their trail. "Hopefully, I left that threat in Dallas, and the police will find whoever attacked me before I have to return."

Bree touched Lawson's arm before he could voice his concerns again. She turned to Shelby. "We're here if you need us."

"I appreciate that."

Paul opened the driver's side door for her. "Do you think you can find your way into town?"

"I can get directions on my phone, and I have your number in case I need it." His was the first number she'd programmed into her new phone once she'd gotten it. "I'll be fine. And I'll be back bright and early tomorrow to start our evaluation, so get ready for that."

"Okay."

She nodded and slid onto the driver's seat. She was looking forward to checking into her hotel and getting a few hours of sleep. After this morning's ordeal, the lack of it was catching up to her.

She started the engine and pulled away. The family watched her and waved and finally disappeared from her sight. She followed her phone's directions and found her way easily into town, where she located her hotel on the square. It wasn't large, but it looked decent enough and had that small-town, homey feel to it. Once she checked in, she was happy to see her room overlooked the square. She needed some of this quaint charm to relax her. The memory of having someone inside her apartment still had the power to make her shudder.

She checked her room, looking into every nook and cranny, wishing Paul were here to take care of this for her, then chided herself for her silliness. She'd left that threat behind in Dallas. Her killer had no idea she was here. She was safe.

Now if only she could make herself believe it.

True to her word, Shelby was back at the ranch the next morning. Her attitude was all business, even if her physical appearance wasn't. He was used to seeing her in business suits and heels, but, today, she was dressed in jeans and her long, blonde hair was down, flowing across her shoulders. The sight of her simple beauty nearly knocked him out of his boots, but he managed to pull himself together before she noticed. She looked relaxed, obviously having gotten the sleep she needed to restore her confidence and poise.

His mom, of course, made sure to invite her to breakfast, and Shelby chatted with everyone before turning the conversation to Paul.

"How do you think he's doing?"

His mom glanced his way. She worried about him, and he didn't know how to convince her not to. That was like trying to convince a bull not to trample you when you got in its path.

"He's good," she finally told Shelby. "He's restless. He can't wait to get back to the shooting and fighting. I try not to think about what he does. If I did, I would drive myself crazy. I'm that way with all my kids. They've all chosen careers that could place them in danger."

He saw Shelby's mind working and decided he'd had enough conversation with the family for now. "How 'bout I show you around?"

She turned to him, her green eyes shining brightly as she tapped her finger on the table. At that moment, he knew the truth. This woman could see right through him, past all the half-truths and avoidance tactics.

He was in big trouble around her.

"That's a good idea." She motioned toward the breakfast dishes. "But, first, let me help with these," she said.

"No need for that," Bree told her. "I'll take care of them. You two go and get started on… whatever it is that you're doing."

None of them really understood what Shelby's plan was.

He didn't even really understand it and he was a part of it.

He stopped by the front door and slipped into his work boots, then took down his cowboy hat. She smiled when he slipped it on, probably amused by the cowboy cliché. But cliché or not, it was something he used to keep the sun off his face.

He opened the door for her and led her outside. "What do you want to see first?"

"How about where you sleep?"

He nodded past the barn to a ridge where the little cabin sat. "That's it over there." It was small with only one room, a kitchenette and a bath, but it had suited his grandfather for years and it was doing just fine for him while he was home.

As they stepped off the porch, Bullet, his black-and-white border collie mix, darted from the barn toward them to rush around their feet. Shelby bent down to pet him and the mutt reveled in the attention. "Who is this little guy?"

"His name is Bullet." They had other dogs on the ranch, but this little guy had become his constant companion since Paul had come home injured. He didn't like to admit it, but he'd grown fond of this little guy over all the rest and liked the company the dog provided him.

She rubbed his head again, then rejoined

Paul on the path to the cabin. "He's very friendly."

"I figured you more as a cat person."

"I love dogs, but cats make more sense when you work as much as I do. Ruby pretty much takes care of herself as long as I leave her food and water. Plus I have a neighbor whose teenage daughter doesn't mind making a few extra bucks by looking after her if I'm gone longer than a few days."

They reached the cabin. He opened the door for her and ushered her inside. "Here it is. Nothing fancy, but it does the job."

She walked around, scrutinizing every corner. "You don't have many personal items displayed."

He had to admit that that was true. No pictures of his family or friends hung on the wall. Material things didn't matter much to him. "My family lives steps away. I see them every time I step outside and speak regularly to those that don't live here full-time. I don't need a photo hanging on my wall to remind me of them."

She looked at him, her eyes narrowing in curiosity. "What about when you're not here on the ranch? Do you keep them on your rack?"

He'd had some photos taped to his rack while he was deployed, but they didn't seem that important now. But, if she was curious... He walked over to his trunk stationed at the end of the bed and opened it. All of his belongings had been shipped back to him after his injury had sent him stateside.

"You didn't unpack?"

"Why unpack when I'm going to return?"

She pulled out a photograph of a woman and turned to him. "Who is she?"

He glanced at the image but couldn't recall the lady's name. Some woman he'd met at a party before his deployment, before the accident. "Just someone I used to know."

Terry had taken that photo of the two of them just hours before getting the news from his wife that had been the beginning of the end for his friend. She'd wanted a divorce, and her request had sent Terry into a downward spiral.

He watched Shelby examine his life, digging into every aspect. If Terry had had someone like her evaluating him, maybe things would have turned out differently. If Paul had told someone like her about his concerns, maybe Terry would still be alive, but at the time, doing anything that might pull his friend off active duty had seemed like he'd be delivering another blow Terry would have to take, a disservice he'd be doing to his teammate. Besides, it would have meant confronting a painful situation, and being a SEAL meant being able to control that pain, push it down in order to focus on the task at hand.

"Why are you doing this?"

"You know why. I'm contracted to evaluate military personnel before sending them back to active duty."

"I've heard your mission statement. What I mean is why are you doing *this*? Why come to my home?"

She closed the trunk, then stood to face him. "I don't believe self-reporting to be an accurate determination of a person's state of mind, especially when it comes to deeply emotional issues like depression and PTSD."

He wasn't entirely comfortable with how that sounded. "So you think everyone's just lying?" he asked.

"Not everyone," she replied calmly. "And not lying, really. But people who are used to packing away their feelings sometimes *can't* give you an honest answer when you ask how they feel, because they don't know how to tell themselves. It happens a lot with soldiers—and serial killers."

He gaped at her. Where had that comment come from? "Serial killers?"

"Criminal psychology was my major before I switched to studying PTSD and its effects on soldiers."

"That's quite a change. What prompted it?"

She didn't respond right away. He figured he'd overstepped the line, but on the other hand, she was digging into his life. He wanted to know more about hers.

"My brother, Steven." Her voice cracked with emotion when she said his name. "He was six years older than me and joined the Marines right out of high school."

He must have been the man in the photo on her desk. The person he could tell she'd lost. "What happened to him?"

"His unit was involved in a helicopter crash that took a lot of his friends. He walked away with a broken arm, so they shipped him home for a few months to recover. I remember I came home from college that Christmas when he was getting ready to redeploy. I could tell something was wrong with him. He wasn't himself. He was moody and irritable and every time someone walked into a room, he startled. I thought for sure his superiors wouldn't let him go back into action, the way he was, but he assured me he was fine, and before I knew it, he was back on active duty. He shipped out with his unit and died eight days later—he overreacted to a truck door slamming and thought they were under attack. He died along with two of his teammates in the gunfight he'd started."

Paul stuffed his hands into his pockets as sorrow washed over her face. "I'm sorry." He'd seen similar things happen, including the incident that had taken Terry's life.

She pushed away a tear that broke through before it slid down her cheek. "I had told my parents I thought something was wrong with him. I'd even gone to see his counselor, but they all dismissed my concerns. After all, I was just a kid in college. What did I know? They took him at his word when he said he was fine."

Now her devotion to her work made sense. "So now, whenever you hear someone say they're fine, you don't believe them."

"Most people aren't *fine*. Especially people who see violence and trauma every day." She looked at him, her lashes wet with tears. "How can you possibly be fine? If you'd accept that there's a problem, then we could get you help. There are coping strategies, tactics to let you process your emotions while still getting the job done. But I can't do anything for someone who says they're fine—who won't admit that there's anything wrong."

She was right. He wasn't fine. He was a broken and shattered shell of the man he'd once been, but he'd been trained to compartmentalize his emotions in order to be able to focus on the task at hand. "And what do you believe you're going to learn by being here and talking to my friends and family?"

"Family knows, Paul. Family always knows."

She walked outside, probably wanting some space between them. He spotted her swiping at her face and figured she needed a moment to compose herself. He ushered Bullet from the cabin, then closed the door. But another thought struck him. What would his family have to say about him? Was she right to think they'd picked up on something even he couldn't see in himself? He felt fine and ready to resume his duties, but a nagging thought kept racing through him.

Terry's haunting last words to him before he'd plunged them all into a battle that shouldn't have started. He'd told Paul—insisted—that he was fine.

Shelby walked toward the barn and to the corral where four horses were penned. One of them eased toward her as she passed by, and she reached out and stroked its nose. "Hey there, girl. How are you doing?" The animal's dark brown coat reminded Shelby of her childhood horse, Penny.

"You ride?" Paul asked.

"I used to, but after my brother died, it became less important to me. I lost the joy it once brought me."

"And you never picked it back up?"

That was a part of her life she hadn't thought about in a long time. "No. I was in college, then there was grad school, then finding a job and partnering up with David to build my practice. There just never seemed to be time."

"Sounds like you work too much." His lopsided grin assured her he was joking, but there was a hint of a challenge in his tone.

"I prioritize what's important to me—my counseling and research, helping military personnel." She gave him a look that turned the tables back on him. "What's important to you?"

He didn't miss a beat before he said, "Getting back to my unit."

She smiled, realizing she should have anticipated that answer. "Now you're the one who sounds like a workaholic."

"I love what I do. There's nothing wrong with that, is there? I'm well trained and I enjoy being a SEAL." He motioned toward the open landscape that lay beyond the corrals. "There isn't much call around here for infiltrating a compound, sharpshooting or rescuing hostages."

It sounded like a typical adrenaline-junkie response, but the longing in his expression told her there was more. He wasn't in it for the thrill. "But there have been times those skills have come in handy around here, haven't there?" Because it had been related to his leg injury, he'd told her about the incident with his brother Miles's now-wife being targeted by a mob assassin, and during breakfast, Bree had gushed about how instrumental Paul had been in rescuing her and her sister from a drug cartel. It seemed having a well-trained SEAL around was always a good idea.

He waved her words away. "Those were

isolated events. I was glad to be able to help, but the rest of the time, I'm just stuck here in the middle-of-nowhere, Texas. God didn't put this desire in my heart to help people for me to remain here and waste my training."

She bristled when he spoke of God. If God took such a personal interest in everyone's life, why hadn't He saved her brother? Why hadn't He even let *her* save him? She'd tried to prevent it, tried to make people take notice, but she hadn't been able to change anything, despite her prayers. "So you feel useless here?"

"I do, often. It's my home and I love it, but I left Silver Star a long time ago for my dream of being a SEAL. That hasn't changed."

"Even after all you've been through? All you've seen?"

"What I've seen is that there is evil in the world, and someone needs to be there to intervene when necessary."

She was moved by his words. She'd never seen what he did from that perspective. That was the downside of focusing more on evaluations than the counseling aspect of her job. Could she ever truly get to know a person in the week or so it took to perform the evaluation? She relied on therapists' notes and opinions as well as the results of psychological testing, interviews and these in-home visits to make her recommendations. And this home visit was turning out to be very interesting.

"If you'd like to ride while you're in town, you're welcome to the horses. Who knows, maybe you'll find your joy again."

She rubbed the horse's nose and liked the idea of saddling up. Maybe he was right. Riding sounded like a wonderful idea. It had been so long since she'd made time to do it, and she suddenly realized she missed it. "I think a ride sounds like a fun idea."

They went into the barn where he walked out two horses. She saddled up hers, the memory of the enjoyment she used to have on horseback returning to her. She'd loved riding once upon a time, when her life was simpler and more innocent.

He walked over and checked out her saddling job, giving his nod of approval before leading them outside. She climbed onto the horse and a familiar sensation swept over her. This wasn't Penny and she wasn't sixteen anymore, but she grew excited about the ride. She had good memories of her days in the saddle. This was just what she needed to get her mind off the attacks and the danger waiting for her back in Dallas.

Paul climbed onto his mount. "We'll take it easy at first, until I'm sure you know what you're doing."

"You don't trust me?"

"I don't accept self-reporting when it comes to horses and guns." He gave her a smug look and she giggled at the way he'd turned her own words against her. It wasn't a bad policy to have, though, since she was certain some people were quick to believe they knew all about horses just from watching them on television.

Well, she was no amateur and she would show him. She led the horse along behind him. After several minutes, probably once she'd proven herself capable of managing the animal, he opened up his horse to an easy canter and she followed along. She wanted to let loose in a run, already anxious for the feel of the wind in her hair, but she didn't do it. She wasn't as familiar with this horse as her own, plus she didn't know the terrain, so she held back and followed Paul's lead.

He took it slow and easy for a while, then grinned at her. "Ready to run?"

Excitement bubbled through her. She

pushed the horse on, doing her best to keep up with him. Finally, he turned and slowed in an open clearing. She slowed down too, but the ride had been exhilarating and just what she'd needed. She sucked in a fresh breath. The air here was clean, and she loved the open fields and sky. She spotted a cluster of trees surrounding an abandoned old car and motioned toward them.

"What happened there?"

"That car used to belong to my grandfather. It broke down one day, and he pushed it underneath the trees until he could get back out here to fix it. He never did, and the trees just sort of took it over."

"Why not just junk the car?"

"This is a ranch, Shelby. We don't throw anything out. Besides, it had sentimental value. He once told me that was the car he took my grandma out in, on their first date. He didn't want to part with it. Nature just kind of took over, but it was still here whenever he wanted to look at it and remember her."

His face softened when he spoke of his grandfather. "You must have been close with him?"

"I was. When my parents started having

kids, he built that little cabin away from the main house so they could have the family home but he could still be close by. He was always there to talk to or to take me fishing or hunting. I was fourteen when he died and it broke my heart. But his had been broken for a long time—ever since Grandma Maria died, which happened before I was born. He always had a photograph of her by his bed."

"He never remarried?"

"No. He always said that once you've had the love of your life, no one else would do. He had his family, his sons, his grandkids. It was enough for him."

She stared back at the car, intrigued by his story. What would it be like to find a love like that? A love that ruined you for anyone else? It sounded wildly romantic, and Shelby found herself envying a woman she didn't even know, a woman who had died before she was even born. Did Paul Avery have the potential for that same kind of passion and loyalty inside of him? And even if he did, why did it matter to her? "How come you've never gotten married?"

He shrugged. "The job."

"A lot of SEALs are married. That's no excuse."

He leaned back in his saddle and locked his gaze on her. "I suppose I haven't met my Maria."

She felt her face warm and realized they were getting into very personal information. And while she was here to learn about his emotional state of mind, she hadn't intended to find out while they were on horseback in the middle of his family's ranch. She turned the horse around. "Maybe we should get back."

He agreed and turned around, too, heading back to Silver Star.

As they rode, she couldn't help being captivated by the beauty of this place, and she wondered at his desire to leave it behind.

Paul's brother Josh was the local sheriff for Courtland County. Paul stopped in to see him before meeting up with Shelby later that afternoon. She'd driven back to the hotel to rest and work for a few hours before they got together.

Paul followed his brother around the station, going over what had happened to Shelby back in Dallas. He wanted to get the opinion of someone in law enforcement. It wasn't that he didn't trust Dallas PD, it's just that he trusted his brother's opinions a lot more.

Josh stopped and turned to him. "Are you sure you should be getting this close to this woman?"

He wasn't surprised by the question, but Josh had no room to talk about jumping into dangerous situations. Of course, it was his job as sheriff, but still—pot, kettle. Any one of his brothers would have done the same thing if they'd been in his position. "What should I have done, Josh? Let that bullet pierce her? Let her drown? Let a crazy, masked man murder her?"

"Of course not. But she's evaluating you. It seems to me like she's gotten emotionally involved with you. It could mess up her assessment."

"The last thing I want, besides her death on my hands, is to have to start this process over again. It took me six weeks just to get an appointment with someone who could do my evaluation. I know how important this is. But *not* protecting her was never going to be an option. Still, what does it matter now? The danger's back in Dallas. She's just here for her work with me."

He still shook his head. "I don't know. I'm not sure it's right."

"She's the evaluator. I'm the evaluat-ee. It's strictly professional from here on out," Paul assured his brother.

Josh flashed him a doubting look that rubbed Paul the wrong way. "What are you implying?" he demanded.

"Just that you tend to get involved, Paul. It's a good trait. Don't get me wrong. You saved that woman's life, and that's a noble thing, but it's not your job to save everyone."

He scrubbed a hand over his chin. He'd heard this spiel before, and not just from his brothers. He was reckless. He acted before he thought things through. He was a so-called adrenaline junkie. "See now, that's just the kind of thing I don't want you telling Shelby."

Josh's eyes went wide with surprise. "So, it's Shelby, is it? Kind of informal with your evaluator, aren't you?"

"Well, when you save a person's life, titles don't seem to make that much of a difference anymore."

Josh nodded and continued walking. "Just as I thought. Emotionally entangled."

Paul tapped his fist against his thigh to hold back a sigh of irritation. Josh was not taking this seriously enough. He hurried to follow him. "Look, just tell her I'm fine, and she should have no qualms about approving my reinstatement."

"And what if I don't think you're fine?"

"I'm your brother. You should want what's best for me."

"I do want that, Paul. I do."

He heard the judgmental tone and felt the need to defend himself again. "I'm fine. Honestly. Besides, you have no idea what it's like to be on the sideline when everyone else is in the game. It's killing me."

"There are other ways of settling your spirit than jumping back into action, especially the kind of action you see in the SEALs."

"What do you want me to do, Josh? Strap on a deputy's badge? Write tickets down at the speed trap on the highway? That's not how I want to spend my life. I would die of boredom." He glanced around and realized several of Josh's deputies had stopped their activities and were shooting him looks. "No offense. It's just not the life for me."

Josh stopped walking and turned back to him. "Look, you've taught my department a lot about tactical operations over the past few months. You could oversee a new training program for law enforcement agencies in the area, start your own business, be your own boss."

Paul shook his head. He didn't even bother responding to that idea verbally. That was not what he wanted to do with his life, and Josh knew it, yet he persisted in trying to push Paul into staying in town. "Did Ma put you up to this?" He knew she worried about him returning to his unit, but at this rate, his family was going to ruin his shot to prove to Shelby that he was stable enough to go back to his team.

"No, Ma didn't put me up to anything." Josh threw his hands out in an I-give-up gesture, then headed toward his office. "I'll speak to this doctor of yours, but I can't make you any promises, Paul. If she asks me a question, I have to answer it truthfully. If I didn't and something happened to you, I could never forgive myself for that."

Paul rubbed the back of his neck. If that was the best his brother could commit to, he'd have to accept it. He understood the hesitation. He'd been in the same boat with Terry, wanting to speak up but feeling unable to. He'd kept silent, and something terrible had happened. He admired that his brother wasn't willing to make the same mistake, but it also frustrated him because of the answers he was sure Josh would give to Shelby's questions.

Only there was nothing wrong with Paul for Josh to be so concerned about. That was what no one seemed to get.

He left the sheriff's office and headed down the sidewalk that led to the square and Shelby's hotel. He spotted her exiting the café on the corner and turned her way. Her head was down and she was reading something on her phone.

A blue sedan at the curb revved its engine and pulled from its parking spot just as Shelby started to cross the street. The hairs on the back of Paul's neck stood on end as it sped her way. It wasn't slowing down. If anything, it was accelerating. He looked back at Shelby, who seemed oblivious to the car approaching her. It revved its engine again, and Paul knew this was no coincidence.

Shelby's attacker had found her again.

He ran, hopped over a bench on the sidewalk and launched himself into the street. He tackled her, shoving her out of the way of the roaring vehicle just as it rammed past, narrowly missing them. He landed first, slamming his knee against the asphalt, and rolled, scraping his arms and feeling the burn of the pavement but focused more on Shelby in his arms. They were already on the ground before she had time to scream.

Tires screeched and he glanced up in time to see the car careen around the corner, then out of sight.

Shelby's racing heart seemed to match his own as he released her.

"What—what happened?" Her voice was shaky and her green eyes full of fear and confusion.

"That car was heading toward you."

A crowd of people gathered around, asking if they were all right. Paul recognized most of their faces and assured them they were. Someone helped Shelby sit up on the sidewalk. Paul sat up, too, but his limbs were stinging and seemed unwilling to move.

Moments later, Cecile Richardson, one of Josh's deputies, pushed through the group, with several deputies behind her. Her eyes widened with alarm. "What happened here?"

"A blue four-door sedan tried to run Shelby over. I managed to push her out of the way just in time. It kept going, around the back of the courthouse."

She stood and instructed two of the deputies to pursue the car, then told the others to start taking witness statements from the crowd. She pulled out her phone and was calling for an ambulance when Josh pushed his way through the crowd and knelt beside Paul, his eyes scanning his torn-up jeans and the sleeve of the jacket that had been ripped by the concrete.

"What happened?"

Paul related the story again as Cecile hung up the phone. "The ambulance is on its way." She knelt beside Shelby, who had gone quiet. "Ma'am, are you all right? Are you injured?"

Shelby shook her head and pushed Cecile's hand away. "I'm fine." She turned to look at Paul and tears flooded her eyes. "It—it wasn't an accident, was it?"

He wanted to say yes. He wanted it to be an accident because the alternative was too unsettling to consider. But he couldn't. He'd seen the sedan pull out of its parking space the moment she'd stepped off the sidewalk. He'd heard the rev of the engine and seen the car aim in her direction as it sped up.

This was no accident. This was another attempt on her life.

She fell into his arms and started to sob. He held her, not even caring about the way his brother looked at him. He didn't care that he'd just gone back on his word about keeping his distance.

Shelby's attacker had tracked her to Courtland County. And no matter what it took, he was going to keep her safe.

FOUR

Shelby placed an ice pack over her forehead as she slumped in her seat at the sheriff's office. She'd bumped her head against the pavement when Paul had shoved her to the ground. Not that she was complaining. Another bump to the head was a small price to pay for him saving her life. Again.

Tears pressed against her eyes and threatened to escape, but she pushed them back. She couldn't break down. Not here. Not in front of people she didn't even know. Not in front of *anyone*. She prided herself on always keeping her composure, and Paul Avery had already seen her vulnerable too many times.

She watched him now, talking with his brother, then he turned to look at her. She took in the tightness in his jaw. The stiffness of his shoulders. The way the sleeve of his jacket was torn along with the bloodstained jeans. He'd been hurt, too, in this incident that never should have happened. She should have been safe here, but she wasn't. He slipped onto the bench beside her and his hand easily found hers. She didn't pull away, glad for the reassurance his touch provided.

"You okay?" He already knew that physically she was fine, but she knew that wasn't what he was referring to.

She removed the ice pack and placed it beside her. There would be an opportunity to talk about her feelings, but this wasn't it. She needed time alone to be able to process it, without all these watchful eyes on her. "I will be."

"My brother wants to ask you some questions. Do you feel up to it?"

She nodded and stood, ready to get this over with and hurry back to the privacy of her hotel room.

Paul held her elbow as he guided her toward a conference room, then motioned for her to take a seat. He slid onto a chair beside her as Josh seated himself at the table, along with the female deputy who'd been at the scene.

"I'm sorry to have to meet under these circumstances. I'm Josh Avery, sheriff of Courtland County. This is my Chief Deputy, Cecile Richardson. You've had quite a shock, and that's a nasty bump on your head, Dr. Warren. Are you sure you don't want to get it checked out before giving your statement? I can have someone drive you to the emergency room."

"No, thank you. I'm fine." She gingerly touched the knot on her head. It mirrored the wound on the other side of her head, but it hadn't bled and didn't need stitches and she hadn't lost consciousness this time. She didn't need to go to the hospital. She just wanted to push through this and get back to her hotel room.

"Okay then. Let me know if you change your mind or need to stop at any point. My brother has given me his account of what happened to you this afternoon. Why don't you tell us what you remember?"

She tried to recall, but everything was a blur. "I decided to go work at the café for a while, setting up my new computer and reviewing some files. I walked out to return to my hotel, where I was supposed to meet Paul." She shook her head as all her memories seemed to jumble together except one—the feeling of being in Paul Avery's arms and the rapidness of his heartbeat pressed against hers. "I heard Paul yell, then a screech of tires. The next thing I knew, I was on the ground and people were rushing over to make sure we were okay."

"So you didn't actually see the vehicle that nearly ran you down?"

Again, she tried to access the jumbled memories. "Maybe for a brief moment, just the grill."

"Did you see the driver?" Cecile asked. "Can you give us any kind of description of him?"

"No. I didn't see him."

Beside her, Paul sighed and rubbed his chin. "Neither did I. The sun was glaring on the windshield."

"I've still got deputies out canvassing the crowd. Maybe someone had a better angle or saw something more. We'll find whoever is responsible. Paul tells me you had some trouble back in Dallas before you came here."

She nodded. It made sense that Paul would have alerted his brother to the situation. She was glad he already knew—it saved time now. "Someone shot at me through the window of my office. The next day, he messed with my car. That night, he broke into my apartment."

"I'd say that's someone who is determined to get to you. Any idea who it is? Old boyfriend?"

"No. I don't really date much. There's no one who would want to hurt me."

"With all due respect, Dr. Warren, you should let us be the judge of that. Sometimes, it's difficult to know a person's true intentions."

"Well, the last date I went on was months ago." Feeling embarrassed by that admission, even though she knew she had no reason to be, she glanced at Paul. "Surely, you don't think he's suddenly fixated on me after all this time?"

Cecile gave her a compassionate smile. "Probably not, but we should check him out anyway." She pushed a notebook and pen toward her. "Why don't you write down his name and the names of anyone else you've been romantically involved with. I promise I'll be discreet."

She saw Paul watching her and her face warmed. Why did it matter if he knew she hadn't dated in a while? "I'm very devoted to my work," she explained, feeling the need to justify her anemic social life.

Cecile chuckled. "Trust me. If anyone can

understand that, it is all the people in this room." There wasn't a hint of judgment in her tone, and that comforted Shelby. She'd always felt like it was odd that she would rather be working than going on meaningless dates with people she was certain she would never see again. Her friends—the few she had—tried to encourage her to go out more, but she much preferred a night in with a good book and her cat over dinner with a stranger.

She wrote down the names of the last three men she'd gone out with, certain nothing would come of investigating them, then pushed the notebook back to Cecile, who glanced at the names.

"I'd like to know about any other enemies you might have."

"I don't know of any."

Paul intervened. "The Dallas police wanted her to go through her files to see if she's had any dissatisfied patients."

"And did you?" Josh asked.

"I had pulled several files before I left town. The physical files were in my briefcase when my car went into the lake, but I asked my assistant, Colette, to email the names to Detective Murphy."

"I can call him and see if they've made

any progress on those names," Cecile stated. "Do you have electronic access to your files?" When Shelby nodded, Cecile added, "We need to look through those."

She'd known their questions were leading to this request, but she was still not compromising on her patients' right to privacy. "They're confidential. I'll go through them and compile anything that sounded like a potential threat. I've already started the process. It's what I was doing this afternoon at the coffee shop before—before…"

"Before someone tried to murder you. Again," Paul ended.

"Yes." She didn't like the idea that someone was watching her closely enough to follow her to another town. Who would want her dead enough to follow her all this way? For that matter, who wanted her dead at all?

Cecile intervened. "Once we get copies of the files from Dallas PD, we'll have a better idea of who or what we're looking for."

Shelby was worn out and wanted nothing more than to go back to her hotel and soak in a hot bath to work out the kinks in her muscles. If her attacker was trying to frighten her, he was doing a good job. "I don't know what else I can tell you."

Paul leaned toward his brother. "You don't think this is connected to the attacks in Dallas, do you?"

"I didn't say that."

"But you're thinking it."

Josh sighed and leaned back in his chair. "You've had someone after you," he said, looking at Shelby before turning to Paul. "And you've been keyed up for months now. Adding that kind of adrenaline to your system has probably got you so ramped up that you see danger anywhere."

"I didn't imagine that car trying to run her over, Josh."

"I'm not saying you did. So far, I've gotten confirmation from several witnesses that the car was definitely headed toward Shelby. But we can't be certain it was an intentional act. Maybe the driver was distracted."

"*I'm* certain. I saw the guy rev up the engine before he aimed the car at Shelby."

"You saw this, yet you can't identify him."

"I didn't see his face, but that doesn't mean—"

"I'm not saying this wasn't a close call, Paul, but Dr. Warren is a low risk for violent crime. The odds that someone followed her here to harm her are slim. Isn't it possible this was just an accident that's been blown out of proportion?"

Paul stood and paced beside the table. "Is that what you think? That I've blown this out of proportion? Shelby was attacked three times in Dallas. Don't forget that."

"I'm not," Josh stated, obviously trying to calm down his brother.

This was getting out of control, and she wasn't keen on getting in between these two brothers, but someone needed to head off this argument. "Enough," she demanded, grabbing their attention. She looked at Paul. "I think your brother is right. This was probably just an accident."

"You don't know that."

"No, I don't. But what I do know is that only a few people knew I was coming here. How would my attacker from Dallas even know I was here or where to find me? It doesn't make any sense that he would, especially so quickly. I've only been in town for two days."

"I don't understand how he knew, but he did," Paul insisted. "I didn't imagine that he was targeting her," he said, tossing his last comment at his brother.

Josh stood. "Regardless of whether or not

this was connected to a larger plan, someone did target you back in Dallas. We'll continue our investigation into this incident until we know one way or another. Who knows, maybe another set of eyes on those Dallas records might reveal something they missed."

She nodded. "Thank you, Josh. If you don't mind, I'd like to go back to my hotel now. It's been a long day."

"I can have someone drive you over there."

"I'll take her," Paul said.

Josh glanced at her as if asking her permission. "It's fine," she assured him. She would feel better with Paul than with a deputy she didn't know.

He nodded, then headed for the door. "Be sure to let me know if you find anything in those files that might lead us to whoever is targeting you." He exited the room, Cecile following him.

When they were the only ones left, Paul walked over to her side. "I'll take you back to the hotel." He reached out and pulled her to her feet. "Hey, don't worry about this, Shelby. We'll figure out who is behind this."

She let go of him as soon as she was on her feet and followed him silently to his truck. The ride to the hotel was quiet. As expected, he got out with her and walked her to her door, insisting on checking the room, hand on his holster as he looked around, before stepping aside to let her in. "It's all clear."

"Thanks for checking…and for being there for me. Attack or not, you saved my life again."

"Yes, well, I'm just glad you're alright."

"Do you really believe that driver was attacking me?" She saw it in his expression. He believed it, but his brother had planted doubts. Josh's guarded response made more sense than that someone had followed her here to Courtland County.

Strangely enough, Josh's belief that it was a coincidence didn't bring the comfort she hoped for. The man was a sheriff, and she was sure he was good at his job…but Paul was the brother she trusted, and she couldn't help being swayed by his certainty that danger had followed her here.

"Lock up tight," Paul said as he headed for the door. "I'll pick you up in the morning and take you back out to the ranch. You can ask your questions to my family. Seven o'clock okay?"

"That's quite early. I don't want to put anyone out."

He gave her a lazy smile that warmed her toes. "Trust me, you won't. We'll have been up for a while by then. It's a working ranch and there are a lot of chores that begin at dawn, but you can join us for breakfast after they're done."

"I think I would like that." After today, her desire for privacy wasn't high on her priority list. She would appreciate the company of his family and the fresh air the ranch provided. Maybe she would even talk him into another horse ride.

He tipped his hat to her. "'Til tomorrow."

She locked the door behind him as he left. She hadn't eaten any lunch, but she wasn't hungry, and she was certain this night was going to be another long, lonely, sleepless one.

Paul awoke early and quickly dressed. He headed to the barn to feed the horses before he drove into town to pick up Shelby. Once they returned and had breakfast, he had a long day of work ahead of him. Aside from the normal ranch chores of cleaning the stalls and tending to the horses, there were several repairs to the roof of the house that needed to be done and he'd been itching to put another coat of paint on the new barn.

She'd come to town to observe him, so he'd make sure she had plenty of work-related stuff to witness today. She'd then get a sense of his usual routine.

He finished with the horses and headed for his pickup, waving to Lawson and Bree along the way as they left for their morning run. He'd gotten used to the ins and outs of life here over the past year. His dad in the rocker on the porch with a pot of coffee beside him and his Bible in his lap. The lovely aroma wafting from the house as his mother started breakfast. The gentle neighing of the horses as they stirred and the sounds of nature awakening all around him.

He did love this place, but every morning, every routine, reminded him that he was away from his team and the career he loved.

He poured two thermoses with coffee from the pot on the porch and spoke a few words to his dad before climbing into his pickup and heading into town. The morning fog was lifting as he pulled into the hotel parking lot and then headed up to the fifth floor.

It was seven on the nose when he knocked on her hotel room door, and she answered after only a few moments. She was dressed and apparently waiting, with no evidence of yesterday's attack, save the shadow of weariness beneath her eyes.

"Ready to go?" he asked, and she nodded and reached for her purse and computer case. "Do you think you'll need that?" He pointed to her computer bag.

"I want to have my laptop with me in case I get a few minutes to look through my files."

She might find some time for that if she got tired of watching him work, which he hoped she did. He didn't favor the idea of having her eyes on him all day, observing and noting every little twitch and bit of frustration he might have. He worked hard, and if he wasn't always polite about it, then, so what? The horses didn't mind what he said. It shouldn't affect his ability to return to his team.

Once they settled into the truck, he handed her a thermos. "Thought you might like some coffee."

"Oh yes, please." She sipped it and sighed in relief. "Thank you. This helps. I was going to ask if we could stop for some."

"I figured you would appreciate that. Long night?"

She sighed and nodded. "I slept some, but

it was not restful. I couldn't seem to turn my mind off. How about you? How did you sleep?"

"Like a baby," he said instinctively.

He felt her eyes watching him and turned to see the incredulous look on her face.

"I've heard that before."

He'd said the same thing to her right before a bullet busted through her office window and nearly struck her. He took a sip from his own thermos of coffee. "I slept."

"How many hours?"

She'd shifted into psychologist mode and he suddenly felt like he was under a microscope. Hopefully, this wasn't the way this entire day was going to go. "In bed by midnight. Up by four."

"That's not very long."

He hadn't even said he'd been sleeping soundly all that time, but she didn't seem to notice. In truth, his sleep had been fragmented and unsatisfying. He hadn't been able to keep the image of that car aiming toward her from his mind—couldn't stop turning it over and over and questioning if he'd truly seen what he thought he had.

Thanks a lot, Josh, for planting doubts in my head.

But no, he was sure—absolutely sure—he'd seen that car taking aim at her, but by her own admission, fewer than a handful of people in Dallas knew she'd come to Courtland County. So how, then, had someone followed her here so quickly?

"It's more than I get when I'm working on a mission. We're trained to go days without a full night's sleep."

She nodded and didn't press him any further about his sleep patterns. Good.

He turned off the road and through the entrance to the Silver Star.

"So what is on the agenda today?" she asked.

"Well, you wanted to see how I handle the stress of ranch life. You'll get a firsthand look at it today. After breakfast, I've got to clean out the stables, then get up on the roof of the house to fix some shingles that have been leaking since we rebuilt the porch after that guy drove his SUV through it."

"That's the incident where you broke your leg, right?"

"Yep. That was it. I was standing in his way when he plowed through our living room."

"Really? I thought you jumped in front of that SUV in order to save your sister-in-law."

"No. It was all connected to her—but at that moment, she was upstairs sleeping. Actually, I heard the vehicle approaching the house and was looking out to see who it was. It really caught me off guard when he didn't stop." He parked the truck. "Guess I'm not as reckless as you thought, am I?" he said, flashing her a grin. It felt good to not be judged for something he'd done. Although he had jumped in front of that car yesterday in order to save Shelby.

He chose not to bring that up.

He got out and led her up the porch and inside. Lawson and Bree had returned from their morning run, and Josh had shown up. The family was sitting around the kitchen table, but there was still plenty of room. It had been built to hold his entire family, but his brothers Miles and Colby along with his sister, Kellyanne, and sister-in-law Melissa and nephew, Dylan, were not currently in town.

"You're just in time," Bree told them both, placing a pan of biscuits on the table while his mother set a plate of bacon next to a bowl of scrambled eggs and several assorted jars of jellies and jams.

Paul motioned for Shelby to have a seat, then took the spot beside her. Once his mom sat, they all clasped hands while his father said a blessing over the food. He wasn't much on speaking terms with God lately, but he'd much rather sit through the blessing than listen to the lecture his parents were sure to give him if he tried to opt out of it.

Once breakfast was over, everyone went about their own business. Bree and Lawson offered to take care of the dishes before starting their day exercising the horses and running to town for supplies. His parents went out to the garden. Josh had gotten a call from the dispatcher halfway through breakfast and had left to handle a potential break-in on the other side of town.

Paul walked to the barn and Shelby followed. She assisted him in letting the horses out into the corral so he could clean the stalls. Once they were unoccupied, he picked up a shovel and held it out to her, but she scrunched her nose at him.

"That's not why I'm here. I didn't sign up to be a ranch hand."

"Neither did I," he assured her as he tackled the first stall. "Josh and I had a few hands we were mentoring, but they all got jobs, so now I guess it's just me." Actually, he was glad to see those young men working at productive jobs and hoped their time on the Silver Star had given them a reason to stay on the straight and narrow.

"You don't like it here?"

"I love it here. This will always be my home, but all it takes to do this job is a strong back and a little muscle. I spent years training and working on my SEAL skills, and I want to use them for more than mucking out horse stalls."

She nodded. "I get that."

He stopped and leaned against the rake handle. "Do you? Is that why you're here spending your days watching me work?"

His tone seemed to startle her. "I'm not sure what you mean."

"I've never known any other therapist who did home visits. What's that about?" She didn't respond right away and he figured she wasn't going to. She had her methods and he didn't have to like them, or even fully understand them. He had only to get through them to get back to his team. He turned back to his work.

After several moments, she responded. "I don't want to be one of those rubber stampers. I got into this line of work to hopefully help people."

He saw the pain glistening in her face and knew her words were sincere. "The way no one helped your brother."

She nodded. "Maybe I'll go help your folks in the garden."

Paul glanced around her and spotted his mom and dad. They would spend several hours in the garden tending to their crops. It was another of those daily routines he knew so well. But he didn't like the idea of her leaving his sight. "I thought it was me you were observing?"

"I can see you from there. Besides, gardening is more my style than cleaning up after horses." She gave him a coy smile before turning and heading out of the barn.

"You don't have to help at all, you know. You're our guest—you can pull out your laptop and get some work done if you want."

"You told me this was a working ranch. Everyone pulls their weight."

"But you don't live here."

She seemed to ignore his last comment as she headed for the garden. He watched her approach his parents, then offer to assist them. He turned back to his work, glancing up every now and then to check on her as she labored alongside his mom and dad.

He didn't understand why she was so eager to pitch in, but after he heard his name and spotted them glancing his way several times, he figured it out.

He was the topic of conversation.

Working with Mr. and Mrs. Avery in the garden brought back memories of her and her brother spending summers with their grandparents. They had always had a large garden. She remembered pulling carrots from the ground while her brother impersonated Bugs Bunny with his "What's up, Doc?" routine. It was a nice memory, but the loss of her brother made it bittersweet.

She looked over at Paul, who was still working on cleaning out the stalls. She sat back and watched him, trying to concentrate on an objective evaluation, instead of noticing the muscles bulging in his arms as he worked.

"How do you think he's doing?" she asked his father, who was working a few feet away.

He didn't even glance at his son before he answered. "Seems to be doing okay to me."

"Just *okay*? He doesn't get much sleep. He admitted that much to me earlier. Is there anything else you've noticed about him?"

His gaze went to her, then back again to

his son. "Paul has always dealt with a lot of things by shutting them out. He compartmentalizes what needs to be done and what can wait. Sometimes, I don't think he ever gets around to dealing with the emotional part."

She recalled the intensity he had when confronted with danger. He acted not out of emotion but out of instinct and reflexes, something he'd obviously learned during his time with the SEALs. "Yes, I've noticed that about him too."

"He worries too much about things out of his control. He's been itching to get back to his unit ever since he arrived home— he thinks they're in more danger without him there to watch their backs. It's been his main focus, so much so that I think he hasn't stopped to enjoy his time at home."

"He is very driven."

"Yes, he is."

"Is that not a good thing?"

John rubbed his chin and sighed, and she saw the conflict in his expression. He didn't want to do or say anything that might jeopardize his son's career, but he was too honest to give a pat answer. "My son is under the illusion that he has more control over this life than he does. He won't surrender control of anything, not even to God."

She didn't bother telling him that she agreed with Paul's decision on that point. She wasn't here to start arguments.

"Do you believe he's ready to go back to his unit?"

"I believe my son is very capable and skilled. He's one of the best at what he does."

"That isn't an answer."

He shrugged, then stood and wiped dirt from his pants. "True, but it's not my job to determine that, is it?"

Point taken. No more questions for John Avery. "I appreciate you being honest with me."

"I will say this one last thing, Dr. Warren."

"Please, call me Shelby."

"Shelby, we raised our kids to be workers. They have to be to live on a ranch. There's always something that needs doing. Paul is a hard worker. He knows how to get things done. Sometimes that means leaving things for another time." He picked up a basket of garden tools and headed toward the house.

Paul's mother watched him walk off, then glanced at Shelby. "So, I guess I'm next?"

"Excuse me?" Shelby asked.

"I heard you speaking with my husband. Is this the place where you question me again about my son and how he's doing?" She didn't wait for Shelby to say yes. "I was wrong before when I told you he was struggling. He's not."

"You want to protect him. I understand that. That's my job too."

Diane made a noncommittal sound and kept her focus on the plants. Shelby let the silence sit for a minute and was surprised when Diane spoke again.

"He never smiles anymore."

Shelby stopped and looked at her. Diane wiped her forehead, then leaned back on her haunches, still avoiding her gaze. "He used to be such a happy boy. He loved everything outdoors—fishing, hunting, riding."

"When did that stop?"

"When his grandfather died. All the joy seemed to drain from him. He still did all the same things, but he never seemed as jubilant. When he joined the navy, I thought it would be good for him. I saw that fire return. It wasn't joyous, necessarily, but he had a sense of purpose and it gave him strength and direction. He was proud of what he was doing." She shook her head and turned back to her vegetables. "Now it's gone again. I don't think I've seen him smile once since he's been home."

"Is he depressed?"

"Wouldn't you be? Injured, losing his best friend, unable to return to the job he loves. Of course he's struggling."

She couldn't deny it. "A lot of people do struggle."

Through the open barn door, she could see him working. He stopped, pulled off his hat and wiped the sweat from his brow, then settled the hat back on his head. He glanced her way and gave her a nod, and she smiled at him.

Everything she had discovered about this man so far showed her that, although he was struggling, he was handling the stress well, but his mother's words struck her. Had he lost his joy? She'd witnessed a few flashes of humor from him, which had been nice, but she wanted to see him really smile and find happiness in his life.

You first.

The thought struck her hard. She couldn't remember the last time she'd been happy. She was content with her life, even pleased with her work and the difference she was making, but she hadn't laughed in a very long time or gotten up excited about the day.

Maybe Paul Avery wasn't the only one struggling.

She spent several hours helping with chores around the ranch, all the while keeping an eye on Paul and his demeanor. Throughout, he didn't seem to startle easily or be overly impatient with his family or his tasks. His mood remained steady, even with all the stress they'd endured.

Around lunchtime, Lawson and Bree headed into town while Shelby took a break from ranch work and focused on her evaluation. She took out her laptop and found a comfortable spot on the porch to work typing up notes about her observations while Paul and his folks went about their day. The quiet busyness of the ranch was suddenly interrupted when the dogs lying in the sun at the foot of the porch leaped to their feet and took off running. She glanced at the barn. Bullet joined the crowd and raced along with the pack, barking and howling.

Shelby got up, set down her laptop and walked out to the yard, meeting up with Paul as the dogs' growls became barks.

"I wonder what's gotten into them," Paul said.

"Do they do that often?"

"Usually not unless someone's coming up the lane, but I don't see a car." He glanced around. "I don't see anything."

A shiver ran up her spine and she felt tension oozing off Paul as the dogs continued to bark. Suddenly, he grabbed her arm, yanking her toward the barn as the sound of gunfire pierced their previously quiet afternoon.

FIVE

Paul pressed Shelby behind him as he zeroed in on where the shots were coming from. They seemed to originate from the top of the ridge, up by his grandfather's cabin. The dogs were going wild and the horses spooked in the corral as several more shots rang out, hitting the wooden slat on the barn, dangerously close to his and Shelby's location.

He pressed an arm against her, keeping her as close to the building as possible and out of the line of sight of the shooter.

The front door of the house opened and his dad emerged with a shotgun in his hand. "What's going on?" he shouted to Paul.

"Sniper! Get back inside!"

Paul turned to Shelby. Her face was white with fear. No way could his brother say he'd blown this out of proportion. "When I say go, we're going to run inside the barn. Okay?"

She nodded with apparent calmness, but the way her hand clutched his arm told him she was terrified. She had a right to be. But they were pinned down and exposed out in the open. They had no choice but to make a dash for it. This guy didn't seem to be going anywhere. Paul waited until a lull, then pulled Shelby ahead of him. "Run! Go now!"

She darted toward the open door with Paul right on her heels. Several more shots rang out, but she didn't stop or slow down. Neither did he. Once inside, he slammed the main doors shut so they couldn't be seen. That would cut off the sniper's visibility but it wasn't a true solution. He'd seen where they'd gone and might settle for shooting blindly, hoping to hit them accidentally. He'd chosen a good location at the top of the ridge. He could remain there for a while, as long as no one could approach him.

His cell phone buzzed and he pulled it out. It was his dad. "I phoned Josh and he's on his way here. Are you both okay?"

"We're okay for now, but if this guy keeps shooting, that could change at any minute."

"Go to the office. There's a gun in the top drawer of the filing cabinet. It's not long range, but..."

"It's something," Paul finished. At least he wouldn't be helpless.

He rushed to the attached office and found the handgun his dad kept there. The magazine was half full. If he could get close enough, he might end this threat against her once and for all.

He pulled Shelby into one of the stalls he'd cleaned earlier. He pushed her down. "You should be safe here until I get back."

She clutched his arm again as he turned to leave. "Where are you going?"

"That maniac isn't going away until someone gets to him."

"How are you going to do that?"

"As best I can tell, he's taken cover on the top of the ridge by my cabin. If I go out the back and circle around the equipment shed, I might be able to sneak up on him."

"That's too dangerous. He'll see you coming long before you get close enough to shoot him. Josh is on the way. Let him handle it."

Paul could see the logic in what she was saying, but the idea of just sitting here rubbed him the wrong way. He wasn't a duck-and-cover type of guy. "He came on my land, Shelby. He came to my home. I can't just let that stand." He hated to leave her, but facing this guy felt crucial.

He hurried to the door on the back side of the barn. Hopefully the sniper wouldn't see him exit through this door. He glanced around, then darted out of the building and up the hill. When no shots were fired in his direction, he figured he'd made it without being seen.

He crouched behind a tree. Pain was searing up his leg and he was breathing heavier than he would have liked. He tried to push the pain away, to stay focused on the task. He had to get to the cabin without being seen in order to surprise this guy.

He took a deep breath then darted across the open space toward his lodging. Several shots rang out to show that the sniper had spotted him, but Paul didn't slow down. It was more difficult to hit a moving target, so he kept moving, pushing through until he rounded the back of the cabin. He stopped to catch his breath.

He was out of the sniper's line of sight now, but he still remained cautious. He was likely dealing with a professional killer, someone who'd already tried to get to Shelby several times. He'd invaded their property without anyone knowing. That meant he was smart and probably well trained. So far, he hadn't been successful in his goal of eliminating Shelby—and, if Paul had anything to do with it, and he did, he wouldn't succeed today.

He wished Lawson was there to back him up, but he supposed the sniper had used the opportunity presented by Lawson's absence to strike. He must have been watching them: further proof that Paul wasn't dealing with an amateur.

He circled the cabin and pressed himself against the wooden structure, then peeked around to find the sniper's estimated location. His cabin was located on top of a ridge, so the shooter had to be firing from someplace close by. Paul should be able to see him from here. Most of the dogs had been scared away by the gunfire but continued to bark and howl from the safety of the barn and corrals. He didn't want them rushing into the line of fire and getting shot, but he wouldn't mind having their keen sense of smell to point him to where this guy was hiding out.

He scanned the landscape, eventually spotting something on the ground. The shooter had made a sniper's nest using branches and blankets beneath the tree where Paul's grandfather had proposed to his grandmother. That tree held sentimental value, and this guy was using it for nefarious reasons. That burned him up all the more.

He picked up a rock and tossed it behind the guy and to the right. The sniper jumped to his feet and spun around. Paul raised his gun, taking aim. "Don't move," he yelled, but the guy turned and fired at Paul, his reflexes even quicker than Paul had expected. He took cover, then returned fire, hitting the oak tree with several shots. But the sniper didn't shoot back, and a moment later, he knew why. He heard the rev of an engine and spotted the guy speeding away on a motorcycle. Paul emptied several rounds in his direction, but the bike was out of range before he even got the shots off.

He hurried over to the sniper's nest where the shooter had left everything behind, including his rifle. Paul's heart dropped at the realization that this was a military-grade weapon. Just as he'd suspected, their sniper was a pro, possibly even Special Forces.

For now, Shelby was safe. The threat was gone, but this fellow had gotten too close and would return to complete his mission.

* * *

Shelby remained huddled inside the stall for what seemed like hours. The minutes dragged on, each second punctuated by neighing horses, the barking dogs and the frequent, terrifying bursts of gunfire. She couldn't remain here helpless. She didn't even have anything to defend herself with if the man who wanted her dead found her. For all she knew, Paul had been shot and her attacker was searching the ranch for her at this very moment.

She crawled to the door of the stall and opened it a little, peeking out—and spotting a pitchfork hanging on the wall. She jumped to her feet, rushed to it, and pulled it down before darting back to her hiding spot. Her heart was pounding as she pressed herself against the corner, out of sight. The dogs began to calm, and moments later, heavy footsteps sounded. Somebody had entered the barn and was approaching the stall where she was hiding. She crouched down but readied the pitchfork in her hand in case it was her assailant.

The hinge on the gate creaked as it was opened, and she spotted the barrel of a gun as someone stepped inside.

She didn't think, only reacted, jumping to her feet and screaming, swinging the pitchfork.

"Shelby, it's me!" Paul jerked and ducked, avoiding the pitchfork by barely an inch. "It's Paul."

It took a moment for her to finally register his words and his presence. She stood stunned and staring at him before she dropped the pitchfork and ran into his arms, relief sweeping through her. His strong arms encircled her.

"I was so scared. I didn't know if you were coming back."

"Hey, I'm okay. We're both okay."

She pulled away from him, and her relief faded to anger. "How could you run off that way and leave me here alone?"

"Staying put wasn't an option. I needed to bring the fight to him."

Anger and annoyance surged through her. He was taking too much on himself—refusing to wait for law enforcement to come, insisting on facing the danger head on, even if it meant leaving her defenseless and afraid, not knowing what was happening…or worse, knowing he could be shot at any moment and waiting for that shot to come.

"I'm sorry I left you," he told her. He

glanced at the pitchfork on the ground before picking it up. He hung it back on its peg. "But looks like you could have handled him yourself."

"Did you catch him?"

"No, but I managed to scare him off. He's long gone by now. Plus we've got his gun. He left it behind." He put his arm around her. She didn't budge from his embrace. She was glad not to be in this alone. Because now they knew the truth with certainty.

Whoever was trying to kill her had tracked her down.

They exited the barn at the sound of cars pulling up. Two county sheriff patrol cars skidded to a halt, followed by the truck she remembered Lawson and Bree leaving in. They jumped out while Josh and Cecile exited the patrol cars.

"Are you both okay?" Josh asked as he hurried toward them. "What happened? Dad said a man was shooting."

Paul nodded. "A sniper. I found his nest up on the ridge by my cabin. I chased him down, but he managed to get away on a motorcycle." He handed over the rifle he'd found. "He left this behind. The serial numbers have been removed, so we won't be able to track the gun, but our sniper is definitely military, probably Special Forces."

"Was anyone hurt?" Cecile asked as the front door opened and John and Diane exited and headed their way.

"We're both fine," Paul assured them. He turned to his father. "You?"

"We were safe inside," John stated. "The bullets didn't come near the house."

Which only confirmed what she'd already suspected. She'd been the sniper's sole target.

Josh motioned to his brother. "Show me where you found him."

"I'm coming too," Lawson said.

Paul glanced down at her without releasing his hold. "Are you going to be okay?"

"We'll take her inside," Bree said, reaching out to Shelby.

She didn't want to leave Paul's embrace but understood the need to. "I'm okay. Go with your brothers."

She watched them head toward the ridge.

Cecile remained with the family. "I'll need to take all of your statements, starting with yours, Shelby. Are you up for that?"

She assured Cecile she was. She wanted to get the words out before the haze of fright and uncertainty made what was real and what was fear induced indistinguishable. She went inside and gave her account of what she'd seen and heard, then listened as Cecile questioned John and Diane. A half hour later, the front door opened, and Paul and his brothers entered the house.

"What did you find?" their father asked.

"Just some tire marks from a motorcycle that went all the way to the road. He cut some fencing that'll need to be repaired, but it looks like he came and went just past the Sandersons' entrance. The ground there is muddy, but with the motorcycle, he wouldn't have had a difficult time."

Paul sighed and sat down. "He must have walked the bike in as he approached. There's no way he rode that thing that close to the house without the dogs alerting to it."

Josh nodded. "I've already called to have molds taken of some of the tracks, but I doubt we'll find anything from it that will lead us to this guy. I've also gotten Sanderson to email me his video surveillance from today. Those cameras have come in handy before. Maybe they will again today. I'm glad he posted them."

"Me too," Paul said. He glanced at Shelby

and gave her a reassuring nod. "Don't worry. We'll find him."

Josh turned to her. "Have you been able to think of anyone who might have a grudge against you, Shelby?"

She shook her head. "No, but I'm still going through my files. I looked through some yesterday, but so far, I haven't found anything that stood out to me."

Josh nodded. "I need you to really concentrate on those records. I think it's safe to say for certain now that whoever attacked you in Dallas followed you here." He turned to his brother and sighed. "Looks like you were right after all."

"I'm sorry I was." His expression didn't seem to hold any animosity toward Josh for his skepticism, and she hoped he wouldn't blame her for her own doubts either.

She reached for his hand. "I should have trusted you."

He took hers, interlaced their fingers and gave her a reassuring look. "You wanted to believe you were safe."

That might have been true, but she also had been foolish to let down her guard.

She ran a hand through her hair. "I think I'd like to go back to my hotel now." She couldn't wait to soak beneath a hot shower and let the water work out the kinks in her muscles from fear and tension.

"I'm not sure that's such a good idea," Paul said. "Maybe you should stay here."

"We're happy to have you," Diane said quickly.

"Thank you, but I would feel better knowing I wasn't putting you all in harm's way."

Paul looked like he wanted to try to talk her out of leaving, but he must have seen the determination in her face. He turned to his brother, who was quick to offer a suggestion.

"I'll post a deputy outside the hotel for protection."

That seemed to satisfy Paul, who stood. She followed his lead and got up to make her farewells. "Thank you for today... I mean, for earlier, letting me hang around and answering my questions."

Diane held her hand. "You're always welcome here, Shelby."

She said her goodbyes, picked up her bag, then walked outside with Paul to his truck. He was on alert the entire time and she noticed Cecile's cruiser behind them all the way to the hotel.

Once they were there, he walked her upstairs to her room and cleared it before standing in the doorway. "I'll stay outside until Josh assigns a deputy to keep watch."

She nodded. "Thank him for me."

"I will. You've also got my cell phone number, right? Call me anytime. Seriously, don't hesitate. I'll be here."

"That's not necessary. You should try to get some rest too."

"Don't be afraid of waking me. I hardly ever sleep."

His face flushed as he realized what he'd just admitted to her. She hadn't missed it, especially since it was something she'd suspected for a while. Another symptom of PTSD he hadn't self-reported accurately. But she couldn't think about that right now. She was still too shaken from the day's events.

And so now wasn't the time to harp on his slip of the tongue. "Thank you for saving my life again, Paul."

"You're welcome. Don't worry, Shelby. We'll find out who is behind these attacks. He doesn't know it yet, but he made a critical mistake when he entered my county."

She liked this protective side of him and was sorry to see him go.

"Lock this door and keep the curtains closed. I'll call you later to check on you."

He turned to leave, but she stopped him by grabbing his hand. "And thank you for the rest of today too. I really did enjoy myself right up until…"

He nodded and she didn't finish the sentence. She closed the door and locked it, then went to the window and peeked from behind the curtain until he got into his truck. Once he was there, standing guard, she felt better. She was locked inside this room. She was safe.

But how could she ever truly feel safe when she still didn't know who was after her?

Paul stopped at the local café for coffee. He'd waited until the deputy Josh assigned—Deputy Rylan—had arrived and then he'd introduced the deputy to Shelby. Despite having an officer on guard, he was hesitant about leaving her, yet he needed to get back out to the Silver Star with his brothers to find out what was going on in the investigation.

He ordered a large coffee and was waiting for it when his phone rang, Josh's name appearing on the screen. Hopefully, he had answers.

"Did you find something?" he asked. This was no time for chit-chat.

"No. My deputy is finishing up taking the tire prints, but so far, my team hasn't found any identifying evidence. The shooter even managed to evade Sanderson's cameras. Lawson is repairing the fence he cut to enter, and the rest of us are headed back to the station."

Paul pounded on the counter beside him. He'd really been hoping they would find something that would identify this guy. He wished he could do a better job of describing him, but the entire incident had been a blur. The sniper was tall, at least six-foot-one, with quick reflexes and dark hair, but Paul wasn't even sure he'd seen his facial features well enough to work with a sketch artist or identify a mug shot.

"How is Shelby?"

"I just left her at the hotel with Rylan on guard. She's shaken up, but she's strong."

"Good. Meet me back at the sheriff's office. We need to try to figure out how this guy even knew where to find her."

"I'll see you there."

Paul ended the call and slipped his phone back into his pocket. A teenage girl he recognized from church—he thought her name was Dina Myers—handed him his coffee. He slipped a few bucks into the tip jar on the counter. His brother had hit the nail on the head with his concern. How did this guy know Shelby was here?

It was the same question that had been nagging at him too. How was this assailant always only a few steps behind them? Someone must have given up Shelby's location. He'd been careful they hadn't been followed, and although his skills weren't as honed as they once had been, he knew how to lose a tail and how to spot one. He was certain no one had followed them here. Her trip had been moved up abruptly and only a handful of people had known about it.

His gut was telling him something about this entire thing was fishy, and he was determined to figure out what it was.

He heard a round of laughter coming from the corner and spotted a group of old-timers he knew gathered there frequently. They kept up with the comings and goings of people in town and would know if anyone new had been spotted recently. Perhaps one of them had seen their mystery shooter.

He walked over and greeted them.

"How are you doing, Paul?" one of them asked. "Going back to the military soon?"

He nodded and slipped his hand into his pocket. "Soon, I hope."

"I heard that woman you've taken up with gets to decide whether or not you go back."

They were just as up-to-date with their information as he'd expected. He didn't like being the talk of the town, but he'd put up with it for now. "That's not exactly true. Shelby has to perform an evaluation to see if I'm fit to return, but my commanding officer really has the last word."

The men nodded and winked at one another.

Paul slid onto the seat beside them. "Speaking of Shelby, have any of you noticed someone new in town, asking around about her?"

They glanced at one another then shook their heads collectively. "I don't recall seeing anyone around town asking questions," one of the men stated.

Another man, Mac Singer, spoke up. "Come to think of it, there was a fella over at the real estate office when I was in there the other day visiting my granddaughter— she works there, you know. He was asking questions, not about the girl but about your family."

"My family?"

"Yes, sir. He said he was an old friend and wanted directions for how to get out to the Silver Star. I told Alice after he left that it seemed odd. If he was such an old friend, he would already know how to get to the Silver Star. It's not like the location's changed."

"And you didn't recognize this guy?"

"No, I'd never seen him before, but my granddaughter said he was renting a place over on Old Collins Road."

Excitement bubbled up in him but he tried to tamp it down. This could be nothing, but his gut was screaming that it could also be something that might lead them to Shelby's attacker.

Paul stood. "I'm going to need to speak to your granddaughter. Alice is her name, right?"

"That's right. She can help you."

"Thank you, fellas. You've been a real assist." He waved to them all then headed outside to his truck. He pulled out his phone and called Josh.

"I may have a lead on the man after Shelby. I saw Mac Singer at the café, and he overheard a stranger asking where to find the Silver Star. We need to head over to Lakeshore Realty. Mac's granddaughter may have rented him a house."

"We'll meet you there," Josh stated, then ended the call.

He shot Shelby a text before he started the engine, just to give her an update.

This could be the break they'd been waiting for. Maybe now they would find some answers about the man after Shelby.

Paul entered the house, gun drawn. They'd gotten the name Jason Randall from Alice. She'd rented him this cottage for the month and also confirmed that he had indeed been asking about their family. She'd described Randall as a tall, bulky man with dark hair, matching the description of the man he'd seen at the ranch. She'd also promised to find and provide the sheriff's department with a copy of the driver's license he'd given her. It had to be the same guy. He felt it in his bones that this was the man after Shelby.

Lawson and Josh filtered in behind Paul. He was surprised his brother had allowed him to take lead on this, but Josh must have known he wasn't going to take no for an answer. He cleared the kitchen and bedroom while his brothers swept the other rooms. Their shouts of "clear!" reverberated through the small house. A flash of irritation bit at him. The house was empty. Randall wasn't there.

Josh slipped out his cell phone. "I'm going to have Cecile try to find out what kind of vehicle Randall drives. If he rented a car in town, we should be able to find out."

It wouldn't be the same vehicle he'd used to try to run Shelby down in the street. That car had just been found abandoned several miles outside town. Running the plates revealed that it had been reported stolen by the owner.

He searched through the rented home and found a photograph of Shelby as she walked by what looked like the lake near her apartment complex. The stitches on her face—a souvenir from the flying glass during the first attack—weren't present in the photo, so it must have been taken prior to the shooting. Which meant this guy had been watching her for a while. Anger burned inside him at the thought. He opened a folder and found a sheet of paper containing her appointments and schedule for the past few weeks. How had he gotten his hands on this information? Was someone in her office feeding him information? That didn't make any sense. Why would someone in her office be helping Randall? And, more important, how had he managed to follow her to Courtland when that trip hadn't been on her schedule for another week?

Josh walked up behind him, saw the paper and obviously had the same questions. "These are private files from her office. Who could have given them to Randall?"

"It's a small office. Only her, the receptionist, Colette and her partner, David Sloan."

"Any friction between them?"

"None that she's mentioned."

"We need to consider the possibility that someone in her office is involved in this."

Paul hated to believe that but knew his brother was right. "I'll bring it up to her."

"It's possible someone hacked into her computer and got the schedule that way," Lawson suggested. "It's not hard to do for someone with computer skills, especially if her passwords aren't that secure."

"That's a good thought," Josh stated. "We need to get someone to have a look at her computer to find out if she's been hacked."

Paul sighed. "Only problem is it was destroyed when her car went off the road and into a lake. She just purchased the one she's using now."

Josh rubbed his face. "Another dead end." He pulled out his phone and hit a button. "I'll call Cecile and have her issue a BOLO on this Jason Randall. I want to know everything there is to know about him."

Paul gathered up the files. Whoever this guy was, he was good. And dangerous.

Shelby spent the remainder of the after-noon tapping into the electronic-records system at her office and scanning through her patient files. Her mother had always told her that if she was nervous to not stay idle. Keeping busy was a way Shelby combated her frustration and anxiety.

Along with prayer. Her momma had also told her to pray.

But she just couldn't bring herself to do that. Not now. Not tonight.

As usual, the idea of praying brought her straight back to her brother and his last words to her. "I'm fine, peanut." But she'd known. She'd known he wasn't fine at all and she hadn't been able to get anyone to listen to her. Not even God.

The files were a bust. So far, nothing was jumping out at her. She couldn't pinpoint anyone who might want to harm her. She wasn't going to be able to help the investigation or find the person responsible.

But she wasn't ready to cower in fear and she wouldn't put other people in danger. Guilt washed over her for jeopardizing Paul's family. She should have known better than to go to their ranch when someone was after her. This wasn't their fight.

But Paul had been there for each and every attack. She trusted him to keep her safe. She was used to keeping her distance with people, but Paul had managed to get close to her while her defenses were down.

Too close.

She needed to maintain her professionalism, and that meant not getting too familiar with the handsome SEAL, no matter how protected and secure he made her feel.

She shut her laptop, needing a break from the screen. She pinched the bridge of her nose, then walked over and started a pot of coffee in the appliance provided by the hotel.

Music filtered up to her window and she took a risk and peeked outside. The town square below her window was bustling even at this late hour. The restaurants were busy and the gentle murmur of the crowd below floated up to her. It was nice, but it also made her realize just how lonely she was. Even before this nightmare had started, her life had been lacking something…someone…and being around Paul and his family had opened her eyes to it.

She loved her work, but she was ready for something more in her life.

A rap on her door startled her, and she jumped away from the window, suddenly recalling Paul's warning to keep the curtains shut and stay out of sight. Her pulse pounded as another knock sounded. She reached for her cell phone and started to phone Paul but stopped, her face flushing at the realization that she was getting flustered over someone at the door. Would her attacker really bother knocking? And with Deputy Rylan standing guard, no one should be able to sneak up on her.

She glanced through the peephole. A man's figure was visible. She couldn't see his face, but he held up a badge clearly marked Courtland County Sheriff's Office. "Who is it?" she asked through the door.

"It's Deputy Rylan. I brought your supper. Paul dropped it off."

That seemed odd that Paul wouldn't come up himself, but he had mentioned following a lead with his brothers. That must have kept him busy the remainder of the day, since she hadn't heard from him. Paul had assured her Deputy Rylan was a good man. And she was hungry. She hadn't eaten anything since lunch at the ranch. She wished he had texted her but she was pleased he'd at least thought to have food brought to her.

She slipped the phone into her back pocket. She could stand here and overthink things, like she always did, or she could open the door and get some food in her stomach. But as soon as she undid the locks, a hulking figure burst through.

She screamed and stumbled backward as he reached for her. Behind him, she spotted an unmoving figure lying in the hallway. Deputy Rylan.

All the air seemed to leave the room as she stared up into the face of a stranger.

She'd just opened the door to a killer.

SIX

Shelby braced herself as he took another step toward her and grabbed her.

She struggled against his grip, and he slapped her hard, sending her flying to the bed before tumbling to the floor. She touched her jaw as pain rattled through her. "Who are you? What do you want with me?"

"I think you know, Dr. Warren."

He reached into his back pocket and pulled out a roll of duct tape. She climbed to her feet. If he managed to restrain her, she was dead. She had to find a way to escape, but he stood between her and the door, and there was no way she was going to get by him. She glanced around, looking for a weapon to fight back, but nothing stood out.

Hot tears pressed at her eyes. "Why are you doing this? I don't even know who you are. Why are you trying to kill me?"

He ignored her questions, even as he moved toward her. In a sudden burst of inspiration, she grabbed the pot of coffee and slung it at him just as he lunged for her. The glass shattered against his head, splattering the hot liquid all over him. He jerked backward and growled in pain, and she took advantage of the moment of distraction to run past him. Her heart leaped at the hope of escape—but his strong fingers clamped down hard on her arm and pulled her backward, keeping her away from the door even as he wiped away the scalding-hot liquid.

"You won't get away like that again."

She flashed back to the night in her apartment when she'd flung hot soup onto her attacker. She'd managed to escape that time, but not this one. He pushed her to the bed, then straddled her. It seemed he'd given up on the tape. Instead, he seemed intent on silencing her himself, his big hands wrapping around her neck and pressing in, choking her. She instinctively grabbed his arms, gasping for air as the blinding pain sent ripples of fear pulsing through her. If she didn't find some way to escape from this man, she was going to die. Right here. Right now.

She forced her hands from his arms and

flailed about for something—anything—to grab that she could use against him. She felt for the phone on the nightstand and picked it up. It was an old-fashioned model. Heavy. Solid. She slammed it against his head with all her might, mustering a surge of strength that seemed to come from nowhere. Blood sprayed her as the big man groaned, then slumped over her, releasing her from his death grip.

She pushed his hands away, sucking in raw, painful gasps of air. It was difficult to shove the man's weight off her, but she managed to crawl out from under him, get to her feet and stumble toward the door. He moaned again, and she spun around to make sure he wasn't coming at her, but the man remained on the bed, still unconscious. She'd hit him hard, but it wouldn't keep him down for long.

She considered using the duct tape he'd brought to restrain him. But what if he came to before she finished? He was a well-trained killing machine. If she was right in front of him when he regained consciousness, he'd find some way to kill her. Her only protection came in escaping. She had to get out of here now.

She ran from the room, cringing at the

memory of opening the door for him. Why hadn't she trusted her gut and phoned Paul first? She reached Deputy Rylan and saw blood on the floor around him. She stopped to check. He was unconscious but breathing, and she noticed his gun missing from its holder. She couldn't stay beside him. Both their lives depended on her getting help. She darted for the elevator and pushed the button again and again, but it refused to light. With no time to spare, she decided it would be faster to take the stairs. She pushed at the exit bar, but the door didn't open. She tried again. It wasn't locked but wouldn't budge. She stepped back, thinking it might be jammed somewhere, and spotted a wedge shimmied into the opening at the top—much higher than she could reach. Despair flooded her. He'd planned for this. She had nowhere to turn.

She was stuck on the fifth floor with a man who wanted her dead.

She pulled her cell phone from her back pocket. The screen was cracked from her struggle, but when she dialed Paul's number, the call went through. "He's here, Paul. He's at the hotel. I'm trapped."

"I'm close by. Where are you now?"

"In the hallway. He must have disabled the elevator and blocked the stairwell door."

"Where's Rylan?"

"Unconscious and bleeding and his gun is missing."

"Are there any rooms you can get into? A broom closet or something?" She heard the sounds of a truck door shutting and the engine starting as she raced down the hallway. All the doors into accommodations had the typical lock that needed a key card to open them, but surely there was a room for cleaning supplies or towels or something. She found one, and her heart raced as she rushed over to it, but when she tried the knob— "It's locked."

She hated the thought of bringing anyone else into her dangerous situation, but she didn't feel she had a choice. She started banging on doors, hoping someone would open up and let her in. But no one did.

"He's going to wake up and come after me," she said, her voice shaking. "There's nowhere for me to hide."

Calm determination filled Paul's voice. "Shelby, listen to me. You have to find a place to hide now. I'm on my way to you." But would he make it in time?

She ran back toward the elevator and looked for somewhere to hide. She spotted a ladder and vent that led up to the roof. It was her only remaining option. "I'm going up to the roof." Maybe she could yell for help from there or find a place to climb down to safety.

"Be careful. I'm nearly there."

She climbed onto the ladder and pulled herself up. She'd nearly reached the access door when her cell phone slipped from her hand and hit the floor below, cracking into pieces. Dread filled her. She knew Paul couldn't do anything to protect her through the phone line, but hearing his voice had helped her keep calm. Without it, panic was closing in. She took a deep breath to center herself, then pushed through the access door and onto the roof. She closed the door behind her and found an abandoned screwdriver to shove through the latch in a last-ditch effort to keep him from following her, or at least to slow him down.

She ran to the edge of the building, peered over the ledge and shouted for help, but no one seemed to hear her. What could they do to help her anyway? Her attacker had ensured there was no way for her to escape—or for help to reach her.

She frantically scanned the side of the hotel. There had to be an emergency-escape ladder somewhere she could use to climb down. She spotted one, but it ended on the fifth floor and didn't extend to the roof. She slammed her hand against the concrete. She was trapped here. Her only choices were to try to find a place to hide and pray her attacker wouldn't find her—or attempt to climb down the side of the building to the balcony below.

Hiding seemed the best option, although the only place she could see to hide was behind the heating and air-conditioning units. It wouldn't take him long to find her there.

Pounding came from the access door. He'd found her and it wouldn't take him long to push his way through the opening. She had to make a choice. She climbed onto the ledge. Hiding wasn't an option. She wouldn't be killed while cowering in fear, and if she stayed on this roof, he would quickly find her. If she could climb down to a fifth-floor balcony, then maybe she could escape this maniac.

She slung one leg over the edge and searched for someplace to hang on to as she lowered herself down. One slip of her hand

and she would fall five flights, then smash against the pavement below. She pushed those thoughts away and tried to focus on her movements and breathing as she searched for hand-and footholds.

Heavy footsteps from above indicated that her attacker was on the roof. She clung by her fingertips to a piece of brick as she struggled to find her footing. She wanted to scream for help but knew it wouldn't do any good.

Paul, where are you?

The man hovered above her. "You won't get away from me that easily." He took out his gun and aimed it down at her and pulled the trigger.

She screamed and pressed her body against the wall, but his gun jammed. Below, she heard the startled murmur of the crowd realizing someone was on the roof with a gun. He tried to fire again, and she lost her grip and slipped down the side of the wall. She screamed until her fingers found another place to grab hold. She didn't know if she would make it to the balcony before he fixed his weapon, but she had to try. She reached for a railing that could mean her safety, but her hand shook and she wasn't sure she could trust her grip. She had no choice but to lunge for it.

God, please help me.

She took a deep breath and reached for it, finally grabbing hold and swinging herself onto the balcony as her attacker fired again and, this time, shots rang out, narrowly missing her. Relief flooded her as her feet hit solid ground, but there was no time to waste. She hurried to the room entrance, but it was locked. She pressed her face against the glass but saw no one inside.

She looked up as the shooter fired again. The bullet hit the floor, spraying her with chunks of concrete that bit into her skin. Tears pressed against her eyes. He had her ensnared. How was she ever going to escape this madman?

Suddenly, another round of gunfire cracked through the air. Shelby screamed before realizing it was coming from below her. She glanced over the railing and saw Paul taking aim at the man on the rooftop.

She screamed his name.

"Shelby, can you climb down to me? I'll cover you." He fired several more shots as her attacker backed away from the roof's ledge. "Come on. You can do it."

Her attacker had stopped firing and was gone. He was probably now making his way down to this room, to grab her. This balcony wouldn't be safe for much longer. She had to get to Paul before the man reached her.

But now that she was on the fifth floor again, she could use the fire escape. It was easy to reach from where she was, and she scrambled down the emergency ladder until it ended, several feet above the ground. Paul was standing right there, waiting for her. His arms encircled her as he guided her feet to the safety of the ground. She fell into his arms, nearly crying out and thanking God for keeping her alive.

The sounds of sirens filled the air, and she was reminded of the deputy. "Deputy Rylan…is he…?"

Paul's shoulders hunched. "I don't know. I didn't have time to get inside to check on him. As soon as I pulled up, I spotted you and that maniac shooting at you."

She closed her eyes as she realized another person had been hurt because of this man after her.

"Here, let's go inside. Josh is already there. He'll want to talk to you," he said as he guided her to the hotel's entrance.

By the time they hit the lobby, several county sheriff vehicles had pulled to a stop in front of the hotel, along with an ambulance and paramedics. Paul hurried her to the front desk where Josh and Cecile were huddled with a clerk and several uniformed deputies.

"We breached the fifth floor and found Rylan," Josh told them. "He's in critical condition. What happened here?"

"I heard gunfire as soon as I got here, and spotted the shooter on the roof, firing at Shelby, who was climbing down the side of the building."

Josh ordered several deputies to sweep the hotel and two others to secure the perimeter. "He must have gotten out of here another way."

Paul agreed. "He didn't follow her down, but I doubt he's still in the building."

Cecile spoke up. "I'll go check the video-surveillance cameras."

Josh turned to Shelby. "Did you get a good look at him this time?"

She shuddered, then nodded. She would never forget this man's face. It was seared into her memory. "I did. He came to the door, pretending to be Deputy Rylan. He said he had dinner for me." She touched her neck where he'd tried to choke her. "I thought he was going to kill me."

Josh took out his phone and showed her a photo. "Is this him?"

She gasped and nodded at the man's unmistakable cold, dark eyes. "Yes, that's him. You found him? You know who he is?"

"We ran down a lead this morning and discovered he'd rented a house outside of town under the name Jason Randall. The license is fake and so is the name, but at least we have a photograph."

"Do you recognize him?" Paul asked her. "Is he one of your patients?"

She reached for her neck, recalling the feeling of him cutting off her air supply. Although she had gotten a good look at him, he hadn't been familiar to her at all. That was the kicker. "No. He's definitely the same man who attacked me before—he mentioned something from when he broke into my apartment—but aside from the attacks, I have no idea who he is."

"Did he touch anything in your room that you can remember?"

She tried to recall but she couldn't think of anything. She'd opened the door for him. Dumb move on her part, but he'd fooled her.

Then she remembered. "He had Deputy Rylan's badge. He held it up for me in front of the door. I knocked it out of his hand."

"He jammed the stairwell door too," Paul reminded him. "Unless he was wearing gloves, he may have left some prints there too."

"Was he, when he came into your room?" Josh asked her.

"I think he was. I'm not sure."

"We'll dust for prints. Maybe we'll get a hit. In the meantime, we'll send any images Cecile can find from the videotapes, and this license photo, to our brother who works for the FBI. Hopefully, their facial-recognition software can identify this guy." Josh stood. "We will catch this man, Shelby, but we'll need you to come down to the sheriff's office and give us a full statement. Plus, we'll need to take your clothes into evidence. There may be hairs or blood from your attacker on them."

"You should let the paramedics check you out too," Paul stated.

She nodded her agreement and allowed one of the EMTs to examine her while they waited for Josh to finish processing the scene, but when they wanted to transport her to the hospital for observation, she refused. She wanted to remain with Paul where she felt safe, and her injuries weren't life threatening.

As she waited, she tried to process what had just happened. She was grateful Paul had arrived in time to help her, but her attacker had gotten way too close this time. She recalled the terror this man had put her through. He wasn't one of her patients. He wasn't an old boyfriend. She didn't know him at all.

So why did a perfect stranger want her dead?

By the time morning arrived, Paul had spent hours stationed outside Josh's office door where his brother had let Shelby have the couch to rest. He'd tried again to convince her to go to the hospital, but she'd refused to leave. She looked so fragile and beaten down. His heart ached to see her that way. She'd had a close call, too close, and he shuddered to think what might have happened to her if he hadn't arrived at the hotel in time.

The idea that this maniac had gotten close enough to her to walk into her room worried him. This guy was clever and well trained. And he was clearly determined. He wouldn't stop.

He spotted Josh and Cecile entering, carrying evidence boxes. They stopped to talk to Paul. "How is she holding up?"

Paul nodded toward her. "She's strong. She'll make it through. What did you find?"

"Not much. A few partial prints, but we don't know yet if they'll be enough to make an identification."

"It's a hotel. How do you know they're his prints and not someone else's? Where did you find them?"

"We found one on the door leading to the roof. Plus, we found prints at the rental house."

Cecile stepped around him. "I took the liberty of packing Shelby's bags for her and grabbing her purse and laptop." She handed him the bag and computer case, and he thanked her for taking care of it. Shelby couldn't go back to that room, not after this. Not only was it a crime scene, but the hotel as a whole had proven to be a soft target, even with a deputy at her door. She wasn't safe there. Hopefully, he could convince her not to return at all but to take refuge at the Silver Star.

"Have you had the opportunity to ask her about her coworkers yet? If they might be involved?"

Paul remembered the schedule they'd found in Randall's rental home. He shook his head. "Not yet, but I will."

He headed for the door and pushed it open. Shelby sat up and rubbed her eyes. The lateness of the hour when she'd retired plus the night's events had her weary. She needed to rest, but he doubted she would be able to sleep very soundly.

"Cecile brought your things from the hotel."

She stood and took the bag and computer from him. "Thank her for me. Is there any news?"

"They collected some evidence, but it's going to take a while to run everything and see if they get any hits."

She sighed and sat down, and he saw his opening. "You remember when we told you we raided a rental house earlier that Randall leased when he came to town?"

"I do. Did you find anything?"

He nodded. "Josh said they recovered some prints, but we also found copies of your schedule, taken from your computer."

Her eyes widened in surprise. "How could he have gotten that?"

"Is it possible someone in your office is

behind this? They would have access to your calendar."

She shook her head vehemently. "No way. Neither David nor Colette would be involved in something like this."

"Are you sure? How else would Randall have gotten ahold of your schedule?"

She locked eyes with him, all her weariness showing through on her face. "I don't know, but I'm sure they're not involved. Neither of them has a reason to want me dead."

He didn't bother reminding her that her life was still in danger, so clearly *someone* had a reason—someone they wouldn't be able to identify if she refused to see that anyone could be a suspect. "Why don't you stretch out on the couch and try to get some more rest."

She rubbed her eyes but shook her head. "I've tried, but I can't fall asleep. I can't stop replaying it in my head. Why did I open the door and let him inside?"

"He fooled you. That's not your fault. You thought you were safe, and you should have been. I hope you'll reconsider coming to stay at the Silver Star."

She shook her head. "No, I can't do that."

"You can't remain at the hotel, Shelby. He

knows you're there and he's proven that he can get to you."

"I won't put your family at risk that way."

"My family isn't helpless. We know how to protect ourselves. And you. Right now, the ranch is the best place for you."

"Really? Even after someone sneaked on and tried to shoot me?"

Her comment stung, but he shouldered it. She was right. He'd let her down then, but that wouldn't happen again. "I know it's frightening, but we'll start patrolling the perimeter and will institute some security measures. You will be safe there."

"I'm sure that's what you told your sisters-in-law, too, when they were in trouble. 'Come stay at the ranch. You'll be safe.' Then they were both nearly killed. *You* were nearly killed when that SUV came barreling through your house."

She was tired and lashing out, but he still stiffened as her accusation hit its target. He couldn't deny that there had been times when the Silver Star wasn't secure enough to keep danger fully at bay. "Well, they're still alive, aren't they? And so are you. Their attackers may have tried to get at them at the ranch, but they didn't succeed, because as a family, we stick together."

"That's not true. You said Melissa was kidnapped by the man who drove his SUV into the house. You couldn't save her."

"We *did* save her."

"Not from being kidnapped. She had to be rescued later."

He rubbed his face. "The important thing is she's fine. The bad guys didn't win. And they won't win in this situation cither." He reached for her hand and held it. "Now that he's proven he knows where we live, we're already taking extra precautions around the ranch. And if you agree to come, we'll amp up security measures and patrols. He won't be able to get to you there again. I promise I will keep you safe."

She looked at him and he could see she wanted to give in and say yes. He pressed his forehead against hers and tried again. "Please, Shelby. We can protect you so much better at the Silver Star. Please say you'll come and stay there."

She sighed and placed her hand on his chest, but before she could respond, an alarm sounded.

He glanced out the office window and spotted a rush of activity. He stopped Deputy Thomas as he passed. "What's happening?"

"Dispatch just received a call about a bomb threat in the courthouse. We're evacuating." He headed toward the cells in the back to clear them. Paul understood the urgency. The sheriff's office was adjacent to the courthouse, added on nearly sixty years earlier for the sake of convenience. They housed the prisoners who were being tried as well as those waiting to be taken to the state prison.

People were hurrying out. So far no one was panicking, but he saw apprehension on their faces. Shelby's face held the same fear. Was this another attack on her? Would her assailant stoop to blowing up an entire courthouse just to get to her?

He found his brother and headed over. "What happened?"

"We received an anonymous call about a bomb in the building."

"Did they say where?"

"No, but we have deputies searching it."

"Do you think this has to do with Shelby?"

"It would be a real coincidence if it didn't. Be alert. This could be a ruse to force her into the open. Head straight to your vehicle and get her out of here."

Paul ushered her outside, where a crowd had gathered on the courtyard lawn. He slipped his gun from his holster and held it, ready to be used if necessary. He wasn't taking any risks with her safety. The assailant had left his rifle behind at the ranch but had brought another one for the attack at the hotel. He'd obviously come prepared to finish the job.

Suddenly, a glare hit him from the bank clock and a glint of light flashed from the rooftop of another building across the street. He pulled Shelby down to the ground. "Sniper," he shouted just as the shots rang out.

SEVEN

People in the crowd of bystanders screamed and fled. Paul pulled Shelby behind a tree for cover. The gunfire continued for several moments.

He spotted Josh and Cecile at the doorway of the courthouse entrance, surveying the rooftops. "He's on the roof of the furniture-store building," Paul shouted to them, and Cecile relayed the information to the other deputies through the radio on her shoulder.

Another bullet hit the tree opposite them and bark ricocheted. Paul covered Shelby with his arms as she huddled against the tree trunk. Her shoulders were shaking in fear. "We'll get through this," he promised her.

"How? He's got us pinned down." She glanced at the weapon in his hand. "Why aren't you firing back?"

"It wouldn't do any good. My gun doesn't

have that kind of range. The shots would never reach him."

His phone rang. He pulled it out and saw it was his brother calling.

"Hang on tight," Josh said after Paul answered the call. "We'll figure out how to get you both out of there."

"Was anyone else hit?"

"Not that I can see. He was aiming for you."

Aiming for Shelby, he meant. Paul ended the call and slid the phone back into his pocket. "They're figuring out a way to get to us."

She nodded, but she was still trembling. Her body was tight and her legs were curled up to her chest. He slid his arm around her. "We're safe for now. We're out of his line of sight."

"How long will he stay there?"

Until he kills us was the first answer that popped into his head. No need to frighten her more so he kept his thoughts to himself. "Josh is sending someone to capture him right now."

"But he won't be able to, will he? This guy has fooled us all multiple times, hasn't he? He's gotten the better of us." Tears slipped from her eyes. "He called in the threat, didn't he? To get me out of the building?"

He nodded. He didn't have to voice his opinion. They both knew it was true. This attacker was shrewd.

They remained huddled together for several minutes, until two deputies pulled a large garbage bin around the corner to block the line of fire. Paul pushed her behind it, then crouched down, and they followed the deputies back to the door of the courthouse. The sniper fired several shots, but they hit the bin instead of them.

Once safely back inside the building, Paul pulled his brother aside. "What's the status?"

"I've got Wesley and Manor at the furniture store." He turned on his radio and listened as the men moved up to the roof of the building, Manor documenting their actions.

"We're breaching the rooftop door now."

The sounds of them bursting through the access vibrated from the radio, along with their shouts at the sniper to stand down. A moment later, gunfire from both the radio and across the street filled the air.

The crowd rushed to the windows, and Paul joined them.

"Manor? What's happening?" Josh demanded through the radio.

Silence filled the airwaves for several moments, except for the gunfire that told them all they needed to know. The deputies were in a fight for their lives.

Moments later, heavy breathing sounded, followed by a deep voice that sent shivers of anger through Paul.

"No one else needs to get hurt. Send the girl out."

Shelby cried out, then covered her mouth with her hand, her eyes green pools of unshed, fearful tears. Paul pulled her into his arms and she buried her face in his shoulder.

Josh put the radio to his mouth and pushed the button. "That's not going to happen. Why don't you come down here and let's talk about it."

The voice on the radio laughed. "You have more pressing duties, Sheriff. Your men are down."

Josh's jawline tensed as the radio went silent. "Manor? Wesley? Anyone copy?" No one responded and Paul saw a look of dread fill his brother's face.

Josh shook his head. "I'm going over there."

"I'm going with you," Cecile stated.

"No," Josh told her. "You stay here and keep this scene in order."

Paul pulled away from Shelby. "I'm coming too."

She gripped his arm. "No, Paul, please don't go."

"I need to find out who this guy is and why he's after you. Don't worry. You'll be safe here. Just remain inside with everyone else."

"But what about the bomb threat?" someone in the crowd asked. "Are we still in danger?"

Cecile raised her hands in the air and motioned to everyone to quiet down. "We've had deputies search the building. There is no evidence of a bomb. At this time, we believe the threat was a trick in order to get us outside so the sniper could get at his target. We don't believe there's any danger remaining here."

He took Shelby's hand and walked over to Cecile. "Keep an eye on her, will you?"

Cecile nodded. "She'll be fine."

He hurried with Josh and Lawson to the back tactical room and suited up in protective gear. He could see Josh was worried about his deputies, and he had reason to be. Paul was worried, too, about Shelby and leaving her behind, but he tucked that worry away to concentrate on what needed to be done. He was trained for missions like this, and two of Josh's men were already down. Cecile would make sure that the crowd didn't turn on Shelby while Paul brought this guy to justice so that Shelby could finally be safe.

Josh, Paul and Lawson exited the sheriff's office through the back doors and sneaked around the buildings in a circular pattern.

There had been no gunfire in a while, but that didn't mean the shooter wasn't there watching, especially since Josh's deputies still hadn't responded to his radio calls. Paul darted across the street. No gunshot sounded. He glanced at the rooftop and saw no one. He motioned for Josh, then Lawson to follow behind as he entered the store.

He hurried up the back steps to the roof of the building. The door was unlocked, and he barreled through, with his weapon raised and all his senses on alert for danger. Josh and Lawson were on his heels, each ready to fire, as well. Paul snaked around the HVAC units and spotted two figures on the ground. Josh's deputies. The shooter was nowhere in sight.

"Clear," Paul stated, but he didn't put away his weapon. He kept it ready to use, in case the man emerged again. Just to be certain, he checked the ledges for where someone could be hiding while Josh and Lawson ran to the fallen deputies.

Josh spoke into his radio. "We need an ambulance. Officers down."

"Are they alive?" Paul asked.

Lawson nodded. "Manor is breathing, but he's been shot. Looks like the bullet went through. Plus, he's got a gash on his head. Randall must have knocked him unconscious." He turned to the other deputy and examined him. "Wesley's not in as good of shape. He needs medical attention quick."

Paul hurried over and turned the deputy to his back. Blood was pooled on the roof's surface where he was lying. He put away his weapon and went into first aid mode. "We need to stop the bleeding." His medic training kicked into gear. Josh wrenched off his protective gear so he could pull off his top shirt, which he handed to Paul. Paul pressed it against the man's stomach, where Wesley had been shot. If he didn't get to the hospital soon, the deputy wouldn't make it.

The gunpowder on his clothes indicated he'd gotten close to Randall. And he'd paid the price for it. How many others would this guy take out before they captured him? No matter what, Paul wouldn't let him get to Shelby. He would keep her safe at all costs.

The paramedics arrived and took charge, moving the two deputies to the waiting ambulances. Paul walked over to Josh, whose face was grim.

"This maniac has caused untold chaos in my county. I want him found and arrested."

"How are we going to do that?" Lawson asked.

"Cecile is my best investigator. I want her to comb back through all the incidents, including the ones back in Dallas, and the false identity he gave the realty office. If there's something that can lead us to this guy's identity, I want to know it."

Paul knew Josh was doing everything he could to get to the bottom of who was after Shelby. He agreed with Josh's plan to have Cecile go through the evidence again. It didn't hurt to have another pair of eyes take a look. The man had let Shelby see his face, and now, today, they knew his voice as well as his false identity. He'd become cocky and arrogant—but he was right to be. They were no closer to catching him at this point than they'd been at the start.

Josh turned to him. "I want you to try again to get her to go stay at the ranch."

He didn't think it would work; she was stubborn. "I tried earlier, but I'll do so again. Maybe now she'll change her mind."

He walked back to the sheriff's office and found Shelby sitting in the corner by the main staircase. The rest of the crowd had been released, but she had stayed behind.

"How is she?" he asked Cecile.

She gave him a shrug. "As good as can be expected given what she's gone through."

"Josh wants to see you."

"I know. He radioed. I'll dig into everything I can."

"If anyone can find something, it's you."

"Thanks for the vote of confidence. I'll do my best."

She walked away and Paul headed over to Shelby. "You okay?"

She glanced up at him and he saw tear stains on her face. "I will be."

He slid onto a chair next to hers and stretched out his legs. "We were hoping you'd decide to come stay at the ranch. I think you need to do this." He reached out and touched her bended knee. "I can protect you better there."

She wiped away a tear then nodded. "I'll go with you to the ranch. I was going to say that earlier."

He pulled her into a hug. Her body shook with fright, and he thought back to her words about not being safe anywhere. This guy had gotten to her in the sheriff's office. If he could get to her there, he could get to her anywhere.

They had to capture him before he completed his mission to kill her.

Shelby returned to the ranch with Paul and was greeted warmly by his family. She still didn't like the idea of putting them in danger, but it was better than placing an entire town at risk. That's why she'd finally given in to Paul's urging. Her attacker had targeted an entire courthouse in order to get to her. She wouldn't place that many people in danger again.

And Paul's parents were quick to put her fears about imposing to rest.

"We're happy you're here," Diane insisted and her husband backed her up.

"The boys are increasing patrols and watching the perimeters. We'll keep you safe," he assured her.

She thanked them, then went upstairs to

rest. She hoped she would sleep better here, knowing there were others around watching out for danger. Her body was crying out for sleep. She unpacked, then crawled onto the bed and was instantly out.

It was still light when she awoke. She glanced at her phone and realized it was actually the next day. She'd slept an entire day away!

She pushed back the blankets and got up. She had so much work to do, going through her files, if she wanted to figure out who was after her. She didn't recognize the man who had attacked her at the hotel—Jason Randall or whatever his real name was—but he must have some connection to her work. He'd called her by her title, and he was clearly from a military background. Maybe he was the friend or relative of one of her patients?

She set up her laptop, then accessed the electronic-records database and began scanning her files. Nothing jumped out at her until she came across the file for Adam Sheffield. She remembered him, remembered his history of angry outbursts and knew she had recommended further counseling for him. Yet when she pulled up his evaluation form, the recommendation showed she'd marked the box that approved him to return to active duty.

That was wrong, and she gasped at the realization that another person had been returned to duty who shouldn't have been, just like Michael Finley. In that case, David had overruled her and approved Finley, despite her recommendation.

She'd planned to go through her records to make certain Finley had been just an isolated incident, but she hadn't had the opportunity to get very far.

She made a note to check through her paper records for Adam's file to make certain she wasn't misremembering, but she didn't think she was. She didn't often allow herself to become frightened, but this man, she'd believed, was a threat not only to his family but to everyone surrounding him.

It had been over two years since Adam had been to see her, so she hadn't thought about him when the police were asking about patients who might have a grudge. Would he have really waited so long to exact his revenge against her? Besides, what reason would he have to have formed a grievance at all, since she'd mistakenly allowed him to return to duty? She glanced through his file and realized her notes were missing from it. Only the admission sheet he'd completed upon arrival and the approval form were there. That wasn't right. She remembered making notes about his outbursts and his inability to control his temper.

She glanced at the evaluation form again and stared at the box checked for approval to return to active duty. No way would she have checked that box herself. Her original form had to have been altered or replaced.

If only she had her notebooks. She often jotted down her observations during evaluations. It helped her to remember things better when she did. She kept the binders in a box in the storage unit she rented. She had years of them. She was obsessive about keeping them, ever since an audit early in her career had nearly left her without the necessary documentation to prove her charges to an insurance agency. If she hadn't had her notebooks, she might have been forced to repay several thousand dollars, but the notebooks had been record enough for the auditor. Since then, Shelby had been obsessed with backing up her files and keeping those notebooks.

She jotted down Adam's name, as a reminder. She wanted to check her notes to make certain she wasn't confusing him with another patient. Of course, actually checking her physical records would mean driving to Dallas, and she doubted Paul would go for that. For now, she would continue searching through the electronic files. If she found other irregularities, she would make a note of them too.

Three hours later, she had six names on her list. Enough, in her opinion, to convince her that something unusual was going on. Each of these cases was from months earlier, but she remembered denying the evaluations for each of these men. However, the office files showed them all approved for duty. One might be a mistake, two an error, but six? No, something was amiss with these records.

She'd lost her most recent notebook when her car had plunged into the lake, but she still had the ones in her storage room back home. Since the six cases weren't recent, her notes from those men would be in the older notebooks anyway. If she could get to them, she could compare her files with her office records. Based on what she'd uncovered so far, she suspected she was going to discover David had overridden her recommendations more than once, but how many times? And why? What did he have to gain by approving unfit military personnel to return to active duty?

She didn't know, but she needed to find out.

She hurried downstairs, found Paul, who was sitting and talking with Bree, and told him what she'd discovered.

"I really need to see my notebooks to confirm this."

He rubbed his chin, his reluctance obvious. "I don't like the idea of putting you out in the open by driving to Dallas. It's risky."

She pointed to the names on her list. "If these names are any indication that something is going on in my office, it might be the reason someone is after me." The realization that a coworker she trusted might have been behind the attacks was still a difficult one for her to accept, but if it helped convince Paul to risk going after those notebooks, then she would use it.

Bree gave her a questioning look. "How would that other doctor benefit from approving these men against your recommendation?"

"I don't know. I can't think of any reason he would, but the fact that I've uncovered six patients whose evaluations have been altered makes me believe something fishy is happening. These are just the ones I remember. If I can get to my notebooks, I'll know for certain."

"It doesn't matter what the reason might be," Paul said. "If he's been changing your evaluations without telling you, he's up to no good."

"I can't imagine David would be involved in anything illegal."

He sighed. "It's only a couple of hours' drive to Dallas. It's worth the risk. Since the guy who's been targeting you is probably Special Forces, this has to be related to your military evaluations."

"I still don't know him." She glanced at the photo the cameras had captured of him and recalled his face as he'd tried to choke her. She shuddered. She was sure he hadn't been a patient of hers, but she *had* seen him somewhere.

"What are you thinking?"

She shook her head. "I don't know. The more I look at this photograph, the more familiar he looks to me."

He patted her arm. "Try not to think about it. Memories come easier when you don't push at them. We'll leave in an hour. I want to get there and back tonight, before anyone knows we're even around."

She hurried upstairs to change, excited and hopeful that maybe they were finally going to get to the bottom of why someone wanted her dead.

Her notebooks would tell her the truth. It was just upsetting to realize that her records might prove that, for whatever reason, David was going behind her back and altering medical documentation. That, in itself, was fraudulent, but was it possible he was involved in something darker? Something that had placed a target on her back?

Paul drove as they headed back to Dallas. She had a locker at a storage facility, where she kept all her notebooks. They included confidential patient information, so she was required by law to keep them secure—more secure than they would be in a closet in her apartment. She'd chosen not to keep them in the office so the notebooks would be safe even if there was a fire or some other problem at the building.

As for *her* safety…it was risky being out in public but worth it, in her opinion, in order to get the answers she needed. Thinking that

David might be involved in something unsavory was bad enough, but to think he might be the one responsible for the attacks against her? She just couldn't believe it. Or rather, she didn't want to believe it—but she would see where the evidence led.

Paul parked in the lot for the storage facility and Shelby unlocked the door to her unit and glanced around as Paul followed her inside. She hadn't been here in months, not since she'd brought the last notebook to add to her collection. She motioned Paul toward the wall containing her file boxes.

Paul reached for the most recent box and pulled it down, placing it in the center of the room. Shelby unfolded a chair and sat down, then paged through the binders until she found the ones that included her notes on the patients she'd listed. She'd written down six names, six patients that she remembered failing in their evaluations, who had somehow been cleared for active duty when she'd checked the official report in the office's electronic files. Her evaluation form had been altered, or discarded completely and a new one completed.

She found the notebook containing the dates of her appointments with Adam. She pulled it out and went through it until she found the section with his name. She read through the pages and quickly verified that everything she'd remembered had been accurate. She hadn't gotten the names wrong— Adam was definitely the violent, dangerous man she remembered. She would never have passed Adam Sheffield based on her notes.

She rubbed her forehead. Someone had altered her official records and submitted them to the military. It was not only unethical and dangerous, it was also illegal. And David had already confessed to overriding her recommendation once. Had he truly gone this far?

It was one thing to override her recommendation with his own authorization form. It was another to alter her official form and submit it with her name attached. That was fraudulent and dangerous. But why would he do such a thing? That's what Shelby didn't understand. What did he have to gain from doing so? Even if he'd been acting from purely monetary motives, it would have made more sense for him to *fail* more patients than to approve them. The practice could make more by not passing patients and then referring them for additional counseling through their office. It would be an unethical practice but more lucrative.

Paul poured coffee from a thermos and handed her a cup. She took it from him with a weary sigh, mumbling out her thanks.

"Not good news, I take it?" he asked.

"I'm afraid not. My notes confirm these forms have been altered. These men didn't just slip through the system, Paul. They were deliberately placed back into situations that could turn dangerous and, in at least one case, has turned deadly. And that authorization happened through my forged signature."

"So your partner, David. He has to be the one behind this."

"Logically, yes. He's the one with all the necessary access. But why? That's what I don't understand. What is he getting out of this?"

He bounced his leg and she noticed his nervous behavior. "I might have an idea how we can find out. What's the name of the soldier who died? The one who got you started looking into this?"

"Michael Finley."

"Was he local?"

"Yes, he was born and raised right here in Dallas. Why?"

"We should go have a conversation with his family."

She shook her head and stood, setting down her coffee cup. "I don't think that's a good idea. Surely they won't want to talk to me. It's because of me that he's dead."

"No, it's not. You tried to do the right thing, Shelby. You tried to do the honorable thing. If David hadn't altered your evaluation, this man wouldn't have gone back into a war zone."

His words were logical, but it felt like she could barely hear them. Her head was swimming. It was more than just her fear of facing this man's family that kept her from acting. She was watching her world fall apart around her. So many emotions fought for control. Anger. Sadness. Guilt. "This is going to ruin my practice, Paul. It's going to ruin everything." When the truth was exposed, her reputation would be left in tatters. But that prospect was better than allowing people to be killed. It would be a tough blow to her personally, but she couldn't put her wants and desires ahead of the right thing to do.

She felt him step toward her and found his embrace comforting against the assault of emotions sweeping through her. When she looked up into his face, she didn't see condemnation there. She saw compassion and kindness.

He cupped her face, his hands strong yet gentle as his thumb stroked her cheek. His voice was soft and reassuring. "This isn't on you, Shelby. You didn't do this."

That wasn't entirely true. "My name is on the evaluations."

"That doesn't matter. It wasn't you. I believe that. Plus you have proof. It's a good thing whocver is doing this doesn't know you have these notebooks."

"There's only one person who could alter these files, and that's David. He has to be behind this. He must have left my name on the evaluation in case there was any blowback."

"Like Finley. You'd be blamed, not him."

"True. The practice would have taken a hit from his association with me, but ultimately, he could pass the buck if the family decided to sue or the government came to audit our records. The only things correct, remaining on these evaluation forms are my name and electronic signature. But that is enough to make me look guilty."

She leaned into him and took comfort that at least he believed in her. But would anyone else? And what would she do now that she knew how corrupt David had become? She couldn't continue to work with him. She was going to lose her practice, lose her gig evaluating for the military. She'd be left with nothing, because of David's actions.

"Maybe we can track down one of the other soldiers on my list, the ones still alive. Maybe one of them can tell us how he managed to slip through the system. Maybe they bribed David? That would explain his incentive to cooperate."

She used her laptop to access the medical files to gain the phone numbers for Adam Sheffield, but after trying them, she learned what he'd given were no longer in service. She took a shot at reaching out to his commanding officer, only to find out that he'd been discharged.

She went to the next name on her list and learned from Bobby Goldman's commanding officer that he was currently on leave, but he provided her with a phone number for his sister, who might know how to reach him. She called the number. His sister said that he'd taken leave before checking himself into a drug rehab center.

"Can you tell me which one?" she asked, hoping it was in Dallas.

"The Reddington Center."

She knew the place. It was owned by a friend of David's, and it wasn't far from them. "Thank you for your help."

She gave Paul directions and they headed out, hopeful they might finally get some answers.

They found the facility without any trouble. Paul parked, then they went inside. At the front desk, Shelby asked to speak with Bobby Goldman and was told the receptionist would see if he was available. While they waited, she was surprised to see a familiar person exiting a door labeled Administration.

"Colette, what are you doing here?"

The young woman's face registered shock at seeing Shelby. "Dr. Warren, I thought you were still in Courtland."

"We're headed back there in a while. We just came to speak with someone, one of the patients." She noticed the files in Colette's arms. "Are you doing some work for David?"

The young woman flushed. "Actually, I'm doing some work for Caleb Morgan, the owner of the facility. You know I'm a single mom, and he lets me pick up some extra work for him whenever I'm running short for the month. It helps make ends meet."

"I didn't know you do that," Shelby said. "I'm sorry. I didn't mean to embarrass you."

She was actually glad that Colette had the opportunity for extra work. She was probably going to need it when their practice came crashing down. "While I've got you here, I wanted to ask you if you've noticed anything strange happening in the office. I've been doing some research and realized some of my evaluation forms that were submitted aren't the same ones I filled out. Any idea how that is happening?"

Colette stiffened and her face clouded over, probably from shock. "I had no idea."

"I'm worried that David is involved in some wrongdoing."

"I don't know anything about that, Dr. Warren. I only put what I'm given into the electronic file system."

"I'm not blaming you," Shelby was quick to explain. "I've just uncovered this. But you see things in the office that I'm not aware of. I thought you might know something." She reached out for the young woman's hand. Shelby could see she had upset her. "Don't worry, Colette. We'll figure things out. No matter what happens, I'll do everything I can to make sure you'll still have a job."

"Thank you, Dr. Warren. I'd better get back to work here. You won't tell David you saw me, will you? I don't think he knows that his friend gave me this job."

"It'll be our secret."

She started to walk away, but Paul stopped her. He took out his phone and pulled up an image of Randall to show Colette. "Do you recognize this man?" he asked her. "Have you ever seen him around the office or anywhere else?"

She glanced at the image and shook her head. "No. Who is he?"

"The man trying to kill Shelby," Paul explained. "We're still trying to figure out who he is and why he wants her dead."

Colette examined the picture carefully but then shook her head. "Sorry. I wish I could help."

"Thank you," Shelby said, then watched her as she walked away.

The receptionist called to them and motioned to a man on the other side of the room. "That's Bobby Goldman."

Shelby followed the woman's gaze and spotted a man in a T-shirt and jeans walking over to them. "What can I do for you folks?" he asked as he joined them.

She remembered him, recognized him from their initial evaluation, although he had slimmed down quite a bit and wasn't quite as menacing as she recalled.

"I'm Paul Avery and this is Dr. Shelby Warren."

He scowled when he looked at her. "I remember you, Dr. Warren. You did that eval on me a while back that nearly cost me my spot on the team."

"Yet it didn't. How?"

He glanced at Paul, then at her before answering. "What do you mean?"

Paul stepped in. "Dr. Warren says you failed your evaluation. So how did you get back to your unit?"

His eyes narrowed in suspicion. "Why are you asking me this?"

"Because you never should have passed that evaluation, Bobby, but someone allowed you to," Shelby said. "And I think you're not the only one. I've found multiple instances. Now, someone wants me dead."

Bobby's eyes went wide. "Wait, what? Someone actually tried to kill you?"

"More than once," Paul confirmed. "She's

been shot at multiple times, her apartment was broken into. This guy even tracked her down in a hotel and tried to strangle her."

"Please, Bobby," Shelby said. "I know you were unhappy with how your evaluation went. I understand that. But I acted the way I did because I wanted to help you, make sure you'd be safe and stable before rejoining your unit. That's all I've ever wanted for my patients. But now someone's coming after me for that—to try to cover up what's really going on. If you know something…please, tell us."

He turned away and Shelby doubted he was going to tell them anything. Finally, he fell onto a chair and spilled what he knew. "I was desperate to pass that eval and get back to my unit. I'll admit, I got a little out of control when you said you weren't going to pass me. That's when Dr. Sloan called me into his office. He agreed to change the report."

"You must be pretty convincing," Paul commented blandly.

"Not as convincing as the two thousand bucks he demanded for doing so," Bobby admitted.

Shelby gasped. She'd theorized that bribery might be at work, but to hear it confirmed was still a shock. "He took money from you to alter your evaluation?"

"At the time, it seemed like the best two grand I ever spent."

"So he just let you go without any further counseling or treatment?"

"Not exactly. He said I could be treated with medication just as well."

Now the rehab center made sense. "I take it that didn't go as planned?"

"Each time I saw him, he upped my dosage. It helped for a while and then he would need to bump it up even higher. Finally, the bump ups just weren't doing the trick, and I wound up using more and more."

"And he wrote you those prescriptions? There's no record of you returning to see him." Both hers and David's records were kept within the same filing system, so she should have seen documentation of follow-up visits or a prescription regimen in his file.

He rubbed the back of his neck. "I preferred to keep things off the books. And so did he. But once he realized the pills had become a problem, he insisted I come to this place. At first, I refused, but he threatened to reach out to my commanding officer and report me for drug abuse if I didn't check myself in. If he does that, I'm toast. I had to take leave to come here and this place isn't cheap."

Shelby couldn't believe what she'd learned. David was taking bribes under the table for positive evaluations, then using medication to try to treat PTSD with no counseling. It was reckless and incredibly illegal behavior and was almost certain to result in lots of patients winding up in treatment facilities—or dead. Without the proper counseling, a prescription wasn't a solve-all, and many patients would fall into other methods of numbing themselves, including more and more addictive medications, alcohol and even street drugs. It was a dangerous and unethical path to place them on.

They deserved better.

She thanked Bobby for the information, then they left and headed back to Courtland.

He drove in silence for most of the ride as Shelby watched the landscape pass them by and tried to wrap her head around all she'd learned. How had her life come to this? At least she had Paul to be with her and help her figure it out. It seemed David had placed both her and Colette in a terrible position.

"It was him, wasn't it? David was the one who hired Randall to kill me."

"It looks that way." He reached across the seat and took her hand, his touch silently reassuring her that everything was going to be okay. "I know it hurts to hear that someone you trusted has let you down, but you'll get through this. I'll do whatever I can to help. When we get back to town, I'll have my brothers do a little digging into David's background."

She was still having trouble comprehending David's involvement. Sure, she had enough documentation in her notebooks to have him arrested for fraud, without compiling any more evidence, but was that enough to drive him to pay someone to murder her?

Paul pulled his hand away and stiffened. She followed his gaze to a car they were approaching, stopped on the side of the road on the outskirts of town. She felt tension radiating off him.

"What is it?" Shelby glanced at the vehicle. Its hood was raised, indicating the driver was having car trouble, but she didn't see anyone near the car. Paul's concern became apparent. Was this a trap meant for them? But who could have known they would be coming this way?

"It's probably nothing for us to worry

about, but I'm not taking any risks." He tapped a button on his phone and she heard ringing as he gave the car a wide berth. "My brother can send a deputy to offer assistance to the driver."

She spotted movement in the trees as Josh's voice came on the line. Paul must have seen it, too, because he hit the accelerator and yelled, "Hang on!"

But he wasn't fast enough. The car exploded before they could get past it.

EIGHT

Shelby screamed as the car flipped, pushed off the road from the force of the blast. Paul didn't even notice the moment she stopped screaming and went silent. He wasn't sure if it was because she lost consciousness or he did. But her well-being was his first thought as hazy memories filtered back to him when awareness returned.

He tried to move and his body protested, pummeled by the blast. His head was pounding and he spotted blood beneath him. He reached his hand to his head and it came back wet and red. But it was the pain ripping through his ankle and up his right leg that worried him more.

He used his hand to unbuckle himself and fell down, hitting the roof of the cab that was now pressed against the ground. Glass and pieces of metal and plastic were strewn around him. Smoke filled the air, and he glanced out the window to see the abandoned car fully engulfed with flames. There was no one in sight, but someone had to have been around to have set off that bomb at the exact moment they'd driven by. This was no accident, and his gut told him Randall wouldn't just leave the scene without making sure they hadn't survived. He would come see for himself—and if necessary—finish the job.

He inched over to where Shelby was, trying to ignore the pain that shot through him at the motion. He gasped to catch his breath as his head spun and nausea crawled through him. He could move his leg, so that meant it wasn't broken, but that still left a ton of injuries that would slow them down. He was concerned with his head injury. He was having trouble focusing and getting his muscles to work as he continued to edge to where Shelby was still in her seat, upside down and held firmly in place by the belt. He struggled until he managed to hit the button just right to release her. He caught her as she dropped into his arms.

He checked her over, and she seemed largely unharmed. A wash of gratitude filled him for that. He touched her face and her eyes fluttered open, a hazy smile forming in the half second before she recalled the explosion.

"What happened?" She tried to sit up and grimaced in pain. She wasn't bleeding and didn't appear to be concussed, but they'd taken quite a jolt when the car overturned.

He wanted to comfort her and assure her everything was going to be fine, but there was no time for that. "We have to get out of here. Now. Can you crawl out of the car?" He motioned to his side, which faced away from the road, and she nodded and moved past him. Once free, she turned to help him out. He grabbed her hand and bit back the pain pulsing through him. When he tried to stand, he stumbled and fell. His head and leg were a mess.

She looked around. "Do you think he's out here?"

"I guarantee he is. He may be trapped on the other side of the flames, but he'll be coming to check on us as soon as he can." It was a struggle to get out the words. He probably had a mild concussion, but it was his leg that bothered him most. He pulled up the cuff of his pants and saw a gash near his ankle. Walking on it wasn't going to be easy.

Shelby helped him to his feet, then tugged

his arm over her shoulder and took some of the weight off his leg. "Lean on me."

He did his best to move, directing her toward the woods, grateful for her help. He had no idea where his phone was, but Josh had answered his call and must have heard the explosion. He would be out searching for them. Paul just hoped he found them before Randall did.

They pushed through the underbrush, branches and limbs scratching their arms and faces. Paul glanced backward every now and then to see if they were being followed. He didn't see or hear anything, but that didn't mean Randall wasn't there. He'd blown up that car to get them out in the open and vulnerable. Probably, he'd been hoping they would stop to help the stranded driver and that he could ambush them there, but Paul hadn't fallen for that tactic. Still, Randall had managed to render them defenseless.

After a while, Paul directed Shelby to a big tree. "Let's stop here for a minute and rest." He needed to catch his breath and do something about his head and leg wounds. They were bleeding like crazy and leaving a blood trail behind them. Besides, he could hear her breathing heavily from supporting his weight.

He leaned against the trunk, then slid to a seated position as Shelby knelt beside him.

Her face was scratched up, but otherwise, she seemed unharmed. Good.

"You have a nasty gash on your forehead and that ankle is a mess," she said. "We need to stop the bleeding." She slipped off her jacket and he grabbed her arm to stop her.

"No, keep it," he told her.

"I need to stop the bleeding. You're leading him right to us."

"Once the sun sets, the temperature will drop. You're going to want that jacket."

"I can't worry about that now, Paul." She pulled her arm away from his grasp and pressed the garment against his forehead. "Were you able to reach your brother? Is he coming?"

"I don't know. I hit the button and I'm pretty sure the call went through before the explosion. If it did and he heard that blast, you can rest assured he'll be out looking for us, along with half the county."

The rustle of limbs a ways off grabbed their attention. He felt Shelby tense and she shot to her feet. She grabbed his arm and tried to yank him up. "We have to keep moving."

But Paul shook his head and pulled his arm

away. He wasn't going anywhere. "I can't make it."

"What are you talking about? We have to go now, before he finds us."

"Not me, Shelby. I'm slowing you down. You have to go on your own." The last thing he wanted was to send her on alone, but it was the right thing to do. He couldn't run and he would only hold her back, giving Randall the opportunity to catch up to her. "Go and hide somewhere so he won't find you."

She shook her head and knelt again, her expression determined and defiant. "I am not leaving you."

He gripped her arm. "You have to. I'm practically deadweight. He's going to find us eventually. You can move faster without me. Besides, it's you he wants, not me, so you're the one who needs to stay ahead of him. Run as fast as you can. If you find a safe spot, use it to hide. Don't let him find you."

"No, I won't leave you."

"Shelby!" He said her name in a harsh whisper, needing her to understand the urgency. "You have to run. You have to stay alive." He reached out to touch her cheek. Tears flooded her eyes and he wiped one away with his thumb. "I couldn't stand it if something happened to you." He wanted to say so much more, but this wasn't the time or the place. "Now go."

She leaned in and kissed him, her lips relaying all the emotions he was struggling with himself. "You'd better stay alive, Avery."

"Back at you."

She bolted to her feet and took off running, disappearing into the trees.

God, please keep her safe.

The prayer came as easily and naturally as if his heart had always been open to God. Because it definitely was open now—wide open with all he felt for Shelby. He didn't even care anymore about the guilt and shame he'd carried since Terry's death. He would face it head-on, would face any trial if it meant keeping Shelby alive. He no longer possessed the power to do that, but God still did. He was ready to believe in that again.

He scrambled around and found a low-hanging limb, which he used to pull himself out of the clearing and closer to the tree. He gathered several rocks and branches that were in close range. If he couldn't run, he was going to have to stand his ground and fight. Randall would have to get past him in order to get to Shelby, and without his gun, which he suspected was back in the truck, Paul was going to have to get resourceful. He couldn't allow this man to get to Shelby. He wouldn't.

Even if it cost him his life.

Shelby ran, her heart pounding against her chest, until she couldn't run anymore. She stopped and bent over, hands on her knees as she tried to catch her breath. She had no idea how far she'd gone or how long it had been since she'd left Paul. Tears flowed down her face, and she wiped them away. How could she leave him that way? How could she take off? She should have stayed and helped him.

The sharp report of a gunshot jerked her up and she cried out. Had Randall just shot Paul? Anger burned through her before sadness overtook it. Ruthlessly, she pushed the sadness away. She had to hold on to her anger if she had any hopes of getting out of this alive. She needed the focus and determination it gave her, reminding her that she needed to live so she could make sure Randall and David both paid for what they'd done.

She started running again, then realized she was leaving a very obvious trail for anyone to see. She grabbed a branch and turned and started moving the leaves around, covering her tracks. She moved backward and then the ground gave beneath her and she fell, tumbling down and down until she hit dirt.

The fall jarred her and pain riddled through her. For a moment, she couldn't catch her breath. Finally, it returned, and she moaned and turned over, her wrist flaring in agony at the sudden movement. It wasn't broken, but it was surely sprained from the fall. She must have landed on it. Her shoulder felt wrenched, too, and every inch of her ached. She stood and wiped dirt off her as she glanced around.

She was in a hole about ten feet from the surface. Dirt walls surrounded her. She glanced above to where the sun broke in through the trees, casting an ominous light through the impending darkness. She touched the dirt on the walls beside her. There were no branches or holes she could use to climb back up. Above her head was a wooden grate she'd obviously stepped on without realizing it. It now sported a hole through the middle. She'd fallen in a boarded-over cavern or dried-up well. She hadn't noticed the opening because she'd been moving backward.

She was trapped inside this hole with no way out. She would be an easy target for anyone, let alone a Special Forces trained operative like Jason Randall.

She tried climbing up the steep surface, ignoring the pain in her wrist, but with no footholds, she made little progress. She knew she had to get out of this abandoned well before that maniac found her. She had to find help for Paul. She prayed his brothers would arrive in time to rescue him, but that gunshot she'd heard didn't leave her much cause to believe he was okay.

God, I need help!

The plea escaped her heart before she could even push it back. She wasn't going to make it out of this predicament without assistance, and only God could help her now.

Her anger set aside for a moment, she admitted the truth. She needed Him to intervene. To do something. But then that anger and bitterness set in again. He wasn't going to. If He hadn't interceded to save her brother, why would He act to save her now?

She was utterly alone.

She sank to the ground, put her head into her hands and cried.

The truth of the matter settled over her. She should have stayed with Paul and fought with him. She didn't want to die here alone in this well. Even if Randall didn't find her, she would die of exposure or starvation.

She heard the crunch of leaves above her and glanced up, listening intently. She heard movement again. Someone was nearby. Panic filled her. Was it Randall? Or someone else traipsing through the woods? If she took the risk of calling out for help and Randall found her, he would kill her for certain. But if she didn't risk it, she was going to be doomed regardless.

"Hello? Hello, is someone there? I'm trapped in this well!" She listened for movement and heard it again. Someone was definitely there. "I'm here!" she screamed at the top of her lungs. "Help me! Please, help me!"

A shadow moved across the ground above her.

"Down here! I'm down here! Please help me!"

She glanced up, straining to see as the sun backlit the man who stopped and knelt above her, casting his face in shadows.

"Please help me," she said.

He moved and his face became clear. She jerked backward as terror ripped through her. Randall. His face morphed into a smug smile as he pulled out his rifle. "You just made my job a lot easier, Dr. Warren."

She pressed herself against the wall, but there was nowhere to hide from this man. No corners to cower in and no passages through which to escape. This was where she was going to die.

But she wouldn't go silently.

"Why are you doing this?" she demanded. "Why does David want me dead? What did I ever do to him?" Tears flowed down her face, but she didn't wipe them away. Instead, anger burned through her and she pounded on the dirt wall. "Tell me! If you're going to kill me, you owe me that much."

"I don't owe you a thing," he sneered, then raised his gun and fired.

Paul tackled Randall as the gun went off, sending the shot high. He heard Shelby's screams but couldn't stop to reassure her as he wrestled with Randall, trying to take the weapon. He'd managed to hide out until Randall passed. Instead of taking a stand to stop the man, as he'd originally intended, he'd decided to follow him—let Randall track Shelby so that Paul could be there with her and protect her. He'd managed to catch up to him just as he was taking aim at Shelby.

A rush of adrenaline was all that was keeping him going as he wrestled with the hulk of a man. Randall, on the other hand, was at full strength. He jerked Paul backward and swung at him, sending Paul to the ground as he grabbed for the rifle. If Randall reached it, Paul knew that both he and Shelby were dead. He scrambled for it, too, struggling to gain control.

Randall headbutted Paul, sending flashes of light through his vision as he stumbled backward. He tackled Paul and pushed him to the ground, grabbing the rifle and pressing the barrel of it against his throat, choking him. He flailed his arms around for something, a rock or tree branch, that he could use to attack this man and force him to loosen his grip but found nothing. He stared up into his eyes, hoping to find some spark of compassion, some hint of hesitation at the thought of taking Paul's life, but all he saw was a determined focus on his mission. Even if he won this fight, it wouldn't be over.

He felt a bulk in the man's waistband and instinctively knew what it was. He reached for it and fired, sending Randall backward. Randall grabbed his side and Paul spotted blood there. It was just a graze, since he hadn't been able to pull the weapon completely free from its holster, but it had done the job. He jerked the rifle from Randall's hand, and, instead of firing, used the butt to smack him until he went down and lost consciousness. Paul hovered over Randall, ready to continue the fight, but it was obvious he wasn't getting up anytime soon.

"What's happening?" Shelby asked. "Who's there?"

He stumbled toward the well and looked down, relief flooding him to see that she was okay. "It's me. He's unconscious. Are you hurt?"

Her chin quivered as she stared up at him. "I injured my wrist when I fell. Other than that, I'm fine, but I can't get out."

"I'll help you. Give me a minute to secure this guy." He walked back to Randall. He was still out cold. He grabbed the man's pack and dug through it, pulled out two plastic cable ties and bound his hands behind him before searching him for additional weapons. He found a knife tucked into his boot, in addition to the handgun and rifle. Paul slipped the knife into his pocket before tying Randall's feet, as well. He would eventually get loose, but every minute Paul could buy was desperately needed in order to give them enough time to get Shelby out of that well and as far away from Randall as possible. He checked Randall's pockets, hoping to find a cell phone he could use to call for help but came up empty.

He pulled a bundle of cord from Randall's pack and tossed one end down to her. "Grab this. I'll pull you up."

She took ahold of it and he strained as hard as he could. His leg was still screaming at him and his vision had gone blurry, but that burst of adrenaline he'd gotten from fighting with Randall kept him going. His overworked body knew it needed to, because he had no choice but to pull her out if they were going to stay alive.

She reached the lip and managed to scramble out of the pit while he tossed the cord aside. He wanted to stop to catch his breath, but there wasn't time for that. They had to put some distance between them and Randall before he awoke.

She fell into his arms and nearly knocked him off his feet, but that didn't matter as he felt the weight of nearly losing her press against him. He ran his hand through her hair and soaked in the relief of knowing she was still with him. She was okay for now. But she wouldn't stay that way if Randall got the jump on them again. "We need to go."

He grabbed the rifle from the ground and nudged her forward, doing his best to catch up. Finally, she pulled his arm over her shoulder again to take the brunt of his weight. Making her leave him hadn't been a smart decision. He resolved now that he wasn't quitting her side again.

He glanced around, looking for something familiar, but he didn't recognize these trees. He'd grown up in this county and lived much of his life in the woods, hunting or fishing, but nothing here looked familiar. He was turned around and having trouble concentrating now that the adrenaline from his fight with Randall was fading. His head was pounding and he was struggling to orient himself. He couldn't even be sure they were heading toward the road or deeper into the woods. He didn't tell Shelby that though. She needed to have hope. Anyway, if they kept walking, eventually they would have to come out somewhere.

He pushed through the pain, but his hope

was beginning to dim. He glanced at the sky and heard a rumble of thunder overhead and smelled rain in the air. A storm was brewing and they would be out in the middle of it.

They reached a clearing and spotted a cabin he didn't recognize. He pulled out the handgun he'd taken from Randall and headed for the front porch, where he stepped away from Shelby to hobble over and peer in the window. The place was furnished but looked to be unoccupied. He tried the front door. Locked. If they took refuge here, it wouldn't be long before Randall found them. He'd have to board up the windows in order to make it secure.

"Who does this place belong to?" she asked.

Paul shook his head. "I don't know. I've never seen it before."

He stepped off the porch and glanced around, spotting a storm shelter several yards away from the cabin. He headed over there, pulled open the door and glanced inside. Shelves lined the wall filled with food, water and other provisions. Someone had stocked this place well. If they were going to take shelter, this was the better option. He could latch it from inside and there were no windows Randall could break in through.

He glanced at Shelby. Ideally, they'd continue moving, but with his injuries and the storm rolling in, this was their best option. He could only hope his brothers were already out looking for them.

"Let's take cover here."

She agreed and hurried down the steps. Paul climbed down behind her. He pulled the storm cellar doors closed and latched them, then found an old rake, shoving the stick through the handles to secure the doors still further. If Randall discovered them, he would have to force his way inside.

Behind him, a stream of light broke through the darkness. "I found a flashlight," Shelby announced, sounding quite pleased with herself.

He was glad for it. This place was dark, and they needed the light. He took it from her and shone it against the shelves, once again cataloguing the canned food, jugs of water, coffee, blankets and medical supplies.

Shelby opened up a jug of water and tasted it. "It's fresh."

He took it from her and tried it for himself. Once he knew it was good, he chugged it down. It soothed his parched throat. Finding this place felt like an answered prayer. He wouldn't even be angry if the owner showed up and got mad at them for using their supplies as long as the guy had a cell phone or vehicle they could use to get out of here.

But he was more interested in the two-way radio he'd spotted. He pulled it down and tried to use it, hoping he could reach someone. It was even possible he might pick up a signal to the sheriff's office, but after several attempts, he heard no one on the other end.

Shelby settled down in a corner and folded her legs under her. She looked frightened and he knew she needed some words of comfort. "We're going to be okay," he assured her. "Someone will find us."

"They have no idea where we are. How are they going to?"

"My brothers will search these woods from top to bottom. They'll find us." But first, he had to alert someone that they were missing. He couldn't be sure Josh had heard that blast before their call disconnected. If he hadn't, his family might become concerned that they hadn't returned, but even then, they wouldn't know where to search for them.

Shelby pulled a blanket from the shelf and wrapped it around her shoulders. Paul didn't know if she was chilled by the temperature or the situation, and it didn't matter. Either way, he wanted her to have whatever comfort the blanket could bring her. Hopefully, it would help her relax a little. They were safe, at least for now. He didn't know if Randall would find them here, but he didn't think he would be able to get inside. This storm cellar was made to withstand storms and tornadoes.

He was glad that God had led them here.

He paused at the realization. God. Had he really thought that? Was he now listening to the Almighty's guidance? He couldn't discount it. He'd never seen this place before, so it must have been built within the past fifteen years. He would have never found it on his own.

He checked the gun he'd taken from Randall and found a full magazine. At least he had that.

He walked over and lowered himself to the floor beside Shelby. She was shivering. He put his arm around her, and she leaned into him, the scent of her shampoo sending his head spinning even more. It was probably just the head injury.

He needed to formulate a plan to get out of here and back home, but his brain just wouldn't focus. He turned on the radio and listened to the static as the noise from the storm outside started to grow.

"How's your leg?"

He didn't want her to know how bad it was hurting, so he lied and assured her it was fine.

She moved to hitch up his pants leg and gasped at the sight of his injury. "This looks bad."

"It doesn't feel too good either."

She found bandages in the first aid kit and tried to clean and wrap it. He let her. Then she turned to the gash on his head.

He watched her, noting the slim lines of her neck and chin and the gentleness of her hands as she worked on him.

"How is it that I'm all beat up and you walked away from that crash with barely more than a scratch?"

She gave him a wry smile. "I don't know, but I'm glad at least one of us can function."

"I think I've functioned well enough. We're here, aren't we?"

She leaned back and looked at him. "Yes, but I can see it's been a struggle for you." She reached out and stroked his cheek, her touch sending sparks through his nerve endings. "Yet you just kept barreling through. Why do you do that to yourself?"

He covered her hand with his own. "To keep you safe. I will do whatever it takes to protect you, Shelby. I care too much about you to let anything happen to you." He hadn't meant to pour his heart out to her here, now, while they were trapped and hiding out in a bunker, but something about her touch opened up the floodgates for him. He moved his other hand to her face and pulled her to him for a kiss, his heart leaping when she responded. When the kiss ended, she curled up beside him, laying her head on his chest, and he wrapped his arms around her.

Thunder roared and the wind whirled outside, but they were secure in their shelter.

He didn't know if God had led them here or if it was mere coincidence, but he was still grateful.

NINE

Voices awoke Shelby. She sat up and saw Paul was still asleep. But she knew she'd heard people talking. Had she dreamed that? She glanced at the radio on the floor. At some point, Paul had turned it off, so the sounds weren't coming from there.

She listened again and realized she recognized Josh's voice, saying something about a search.

She sat up quickly. They were looking for them, and they had to be right outside.

She shook Paul's shoulders, but he didn't open his eyes. Heat radiated off him. She pressed her hand to his face. He was burning up, probably an infection from his leg wound.

She recalled how haggard he'd looked last night but how strong he'd been, protecting her and guiding her through every danger they'd faced. He'd pushed through gruesome injuries to rescue her, when most people would have fallen. But it had been the honest declaration of his feelings for her that had truly touched her.

She heard movement outside, then someone banging on the shelter doors. She slipped off the blanket and ran up the steps, pulled out the rake and undid the latch, but when she tried to push them open, they wouldn't budge.

She hammered on them. "Hello! We're in here!"

Cecile's voice wafted through. "Shelby? Is that you?"

"Yes, we're inside. We're trapped. Please hurry! Paul needs an ambulance."

"Stand back away from the doors," a male voice said.

She did as she was instructed, and after a moment, the doors popped open. She glanced up. Sunlight poured in through the opening so brightly that she had to shield her eyes with her hand. She had no idea when last night's storm had ended, but she'd never been so happy to see the light of a new day.

"You said Paul needs medical attention. What about you? Are you okay?" Cecile asked, coming down the steps.

"I'm fine. Paul's the one who's injured."

Josh and Lawson hurried to Paul. "He's burning up," Josh stated while Lawson pulled up Paul's pants leg and viewed the injury. Josh pulled out his radio and called for an ambulance.

"How did you find us?"

"We found the car and started a search. The dogs tracked you through the woods," Lawson told her.

Cecile draped a blanket around her shoulders. "Did Paul know this place was here?"

"We just stumbled across it. Did you locate Randall?"

She shook her head. "No, we didn't."

"Don't worry. We will," Josh assured her.

She watched as the ambulance arrived and paramedics loaded Paul onto a gurney. He still hadn't regained consciousness, and that worried her, recalling his head wound.

Once he was out, Cecile led her up the stairs. She flinched back at the sunlight and covered her eyes. Cecile quickly led her to her patrol car.

"I want to go with Paul."

"We'll be right behind him. You need to get checked out at the hospital too."

"I'm fine."

"Sure, but you still need to get checked

out." Cecile opened the passenger door for her and Shelby slipped inside.

She was grateful that the terrible night was over, but Paul hadn't regained consciousness, even with all the commotion going on, and that wasn't a good indicator. He'd pushed himself so hard to keep her safe, even through his injuries, and she owed him her life.

Tears slipped down her cheeks and she wiped them away, grateful to feel mostly safe again.

But even as Cecile drove them into town, she knew this wasn't over. The night had ended, and they'd been rescued, but Paul's health was still in jeopardy. Randall was still out there. David still wanted her dead.

The emergency room doctor checked her out and gave her the all clear. Cecile offered to take her back to the Silver Star, but she wasn't going anywhere until she knew Paul was okay. Instead, Cecile escorted her to the waiting room where the family was gathered. Josh, Lawson and John were all on their phones, but Bree and Diane walked over. Bree hugged her and Diane took her hand.

Bree gestured at the others. "They're calling Miles, Colby and Kellyanne to let them know what happened."

"How is he?" Shelby asked.

"They haven't told us anything yet," Diane said. She sat down and pulled Shelby with her, never letting go of her hand. "When John and I saw his truck early this morning, I was so scared. I can't imagine how either of you walked away from that."

"Paul seems to have taken the bigger brunt."

"Thank you for taking care of him."

"You have that backward, Mrs. Avery. He took care of me. He's a true hero." He was *her* hero, and she would never forget how he'd battled for her or the way he'd kissed her and made her feel so safe…and so loved.

She'd fallen for Paul Avery. He was everything she hadn't even known she wanted in a man and everything she needed.

The doors opened and a doctor approached them.

"How is he?" Josh demanded.

"He's going to be fine. He's sustained a mild concussion as well as cuts on his head and leg. The leg injury was deep, but it didn't do any lasting damage. However, he's already developed an infection from it. We're treating him with IV antibiotics, and he'll recover."

Shelby joined in the collective sigh of relief that filled the room. "When can we see him?" She felt herself flush as she realized she should be the last to visit him.

The doctor looked at her. "Actually, he's awake and asking for you, Shelby."

She turned to Diane who gave her hand a reassuring squeeze. "He's worried about you and probably wants to see for himself that you're okay. Go. Ease his mind."

"But it should really be family first."

"We're fine now that we know he's okay. It's the not knowing that frightens you."

Shelby glanced around at the rest of them, and they all encouraged her on. She followed the doctor through the doors and down a long hall. He motioned toward a room, and when she entered it, she found Paul lying in the hospital bed. He was bandaged up and hooked to an assortment of machines and IVs, but he smiled broadly when he saw her. "Shelby."

The way he spoke her name sent her running to him. She hugged him tightly as the door to all the emotions she had been holding back was flung open.

"I'm okay," he assured her. "Are you okay?"

She nodded and sniffed back her tears.

"Just some scratches and bruises. They've already released me."

"Good."

She pulled up a chair and gripped his hand. "I'm not going anywhere. I'm staying right here with you. I'm not leaving your side again."

He smiled and linked his fingers with hers before leaning back and closing his eyes.

Shelby listened to the gentle beeping of the machine keeping time with his heart rate and felt a peace settle over her. They still had a fight ahead of them.

But for the moment, they were safe.

Paul was feeling better by the next day and was already anxious to be released from the hospital.

Shelby had remained by his side all day just as she'd promised, sleeping in the hospital recliner. He'd tried to convince her to go back to the Silver Star where she could be more comfortable, but she'd refused and he had to admit he was glad she'd remained. He'd meant it when he said he was sticking close to her, and the deputy posted to the door for security had given them both a sense of comfort.

Once he received his discharge papers, Lawson stopped by to pick them both up. He looked grim as he entered the room.

"What's the matter?"

"I was just upstairs checking on Rylan's condition. He's stable, but he's going to have a long recovery ahead of him."

Paul glanced at Shelby and was reminded of how close she'd come to being killed that night in her hotel room. Not as close as Rylan though. "How is his wife holding up?" Rylan had a pregnant wife and two kids under five, so he could only imagine how difficult this was for his family.

"She's hanging in. Her mother came in town to help out with the kids, and Mom and Bree have been taking turns too. The doctors believe he's going to be okay."

"What about the other two deputies that were shot on the roof?" Shelby asked.

"They're both doing well. They should make full recoveries."

"That's good to hear."

Randall had already created enough chaos in this county. It was time to put an end to his reign of terror.

Lawson drove them to the sheriff's office, where they joined his brothers, Cecile and a handful of other deputies to discuss the Randall situation and how to find him.

"We've been brainstorming ways to get this guy out in the open on our terms," Josh said. "We think we've come up with something, but you're probably not going to like it."

Paul's stomach clenched. He already disliked so much about this case. "What is it?"

"We use Shelby to lure him out into the open."

"You're right. I hate that idea."

Josh put out his hands in a wait-a-minute gesture. "Hear us out. We have a plan. We make it known that she's going to be at a certain place, like that cabin with the storm shelter for instance. We can say she's going into deep hiding. Randall will have to go there to get to her, and that's where we capture him."

Paul listened and absorbed the information. Except for the part about putting her in danger, it wasn't a terrible idea. "How would Randall know where she's going to be? If we're pretending she's hiding out, how can we make sure he knows about it?"

Josh grinned. "We have her phone David and tell him. He doesn't know we're on to his involvement yet, so she can say she'll be out of contact for a while and explain where she'll be. If he is involved, he'll be sure to alert Randall, who will then show up and fall right into our trap."

Of course he would show up. They'd already established David was behind these attacks on Shelby, even if they didn't have solid proof yet. He'd told his brother all about what Shelby had discovered at the storage facility and the rehab center, and thankfully, they'd been able to recover her notebooks from the truck after the crash. Incredibly, they'd been strewn about but undamaged. "But Shelby doesn't actually have to be at the cabin for this to work, right? I won't have her put in danger's way again."

Shelby surprised him by speaking up. "I'm already in danger. I'm ready for this to end. I'm ready to get my life back."

Josh stopped her. "We would never risk you, Shelby. We'll use Cecile as a decoy."

"But I want to help," she protested.

"I'm sorry," Josh said, "but Paul is right. Your safety is too important. Cecile is trained to handle something like this. She's done it before."

Paul agreed. Cecile had played decoy last year to find the man trying to kill his newest sister-in-law Melissa. She'd pretended to be

Melissa and nearly captured the perpetrator. She'd done a good job too. With this change, Paul was also having a change of heart about the overall plan. "As long as Cecile is the one and not Shelby, I'm on board with it."

Shelby pulled him aside. "This is my life. If I want to take that risk in order to end this, then it should be my choice. I don't like being pushed out of the loop this way."

"We're not trying to push you out. But Cecile is better trained to handle this. I say, let her handle it."

"So, everyone is allowed to take a risk but me?"

He didn't like to see her angry, but better angry than dead, as far as he was concerned.

"Shelby, this man is a killer."

"Do you think I've forgotten that? Trust me, I know."

"I won't let you take this risk."

"But you will risk yourself? You can barely walk, yet you're insisting on being there. I should be there too. It's me he's after."

Josh intervened. "I'm sorry, Shelby, but we can't have a civilian involved in this operation."

"Paul isn't one of your deputies and you're allowing him to go."

"Actually, he is. I deputized him years ago."

She stared at them each, then gave a frustrated sigh. "I don't like having other people decide my life for me."

Paul pushed away, irritated at her insistence. Did she want to die? "It's better than being dead, isn't it?" He didn't mean his words to come out so sharply, but he wouldn't apologize. She was being stubborn and reckless, wanting to be involved when there was no need for it. But he had to be there. Randall would never believe that he would leave her alone. He turned back to Josh. "Did we find out who owns the cabin? Will they let us use it?"

"It's owned by Seth Rollins. He's been prepping it for an end-of-the-world scenario. He wasn't happy learning that you'd been there, but after I convinced him that some goodwill toward the sheriff's office wasn't a bad thing, he agreed to let us use it one more time."

Paul was glad to know his brother had taken care of everything. He turned to Shelby, who still didn't look happy. "So then all that's left is to make the call to David."

He walked her into the conference room and picked up the receiver from the phone on the table and held it out to her. She gave him a death stare for several moments before taking it from him. "I'm still not happy about this."

He nodded his understanding. She might not be happy about it, but at least she wasn't dead.

Shelby dialed David's number and waited until he answered. Paul stood staring eagle-eyed at her, listening to her every word as if David was going to leap through the phone and attack her. At first, she thought he was being silly, but when David picked up, her heart did a quick flip and her mouth went dry with fear. This man, this former friend of hers, had sent a killer after her.

She cleared her throat and tried her best to keep her voice calm. "David, it's Shelby."

He seemed surprised to hear from her. "Hi. How are you doing?"

"Not too good, David. This man who is after me, he's relentless. I've nearly been killed several times. This past time, he came way too close to finishing his mission." She shuddered, recalling the barrel of that gun aimed right at her. If Paul hadn't intervened, she would be dead.

"That's terrible."

Her nervousness turned to disgust at the false concern in his voice.

"I thought that navy SEAL patient of yours was looking out for you."

"He is, but this guy has been able to reach us wherever we go. There's a cabin we found in the woods. It's very isolated. He wants to take me there to hide out until his brothers can find this man. That's why I'm calling. I'll be out of touch for a while."

David didn't speak for a moment, and Shelby held her breath as she waited for his response. "I think that's a good idea. I know you hate to be locked down, but if it will keep you out of harm's way, I think Paul is right that it's the smart choice to make. You should go as soon as possible."

"We're leaving this afternoon."

"Where is this cabin located?"

"In the woods near the outskirts of Courtland. We found it accidentally yesterday when we were running for our lives. Paul's brother reached out to the person who owns it and received permission to use it for a while. He believes hiding out there will keep me safe."

"I'm glad to hear you're taking his advice. You've been taking this threat against you too lightly."

"I know. I just never imagined someone would go to such lengths to kill me. Why would someone want me dead, David?" He grunted and she waited again, hoping he might accidentally reveal something.

"I don't know, Shelby, but I hope Paul and his friends can figure that out and bring you back safely. We miss you."

"I've only been gone a week."

"Still, it's too quiet around here."

She didn't want to hear how much he missed her. If he cared about her so much, then why pay someone to kill her? Was that guilt she heard in his tone? "I should go. I'll speak to you once this is all over."

"Take care of yourself, Shelby, and be careful."

He ended the call and she stared at the phone, anger bursting through her. How dare he tell her to be careful and safe when he was the one who'd hired someone to kill her? She looked up at Paul, Josh and Cecile.

She still didn't like the fact that her part was over now.

"What if this doesn't work? What if he doesn't come?"

"He will, and we will catch him when he does."

"He might see you all watching and realize it's a trap." She wrapped her arms around herself in a protective manner. This man after her, this Jason Randall, seemed relentless in his pursuit of her.

"He won't see us, Shelby," Paul assured her. "I've worked with these deputies before and I've given them some pointers on blending into the environment. It's not my first infiltration mission."

"It's probably not his, either, if he is Special Forces."

He slid onto a chair opposite her and reached for her hand. "Look, you've set the trap by telling David where you are. If this guy shows up, we'll know for certain that David is involved. It'll be the proof we need for him to be arrested. Once the truth is exposed, there will be nothing to be gained from hurting you. You'll finally be safe." He squeezed her hand. "I won't let anything happen to you, Shelby. That's a promise."

He stood, leaned across the table and kissed her, and she soaked in that promise. She didn't know why this was all happening, but at least Paul was by her side. Maybe the plan would go well and this could be finished quickly.

She wasn't keen on the idea of him leaving and her staying behind at the sheriff's office, but she knew it was pointless to argue. Lawson would remain with her to protect her, just in case things went sideways, but none of them were expecting any difficulties.

She just wished she were as confident about this outcome as they all seemed to be.

Paul loaded up the pickup with things they would need at the cabin. He tried to act nonchalant, but his instincts were on sharp alert for anyone watching. He sensed someone was there and that the shooter was observing and waiting for his opportunity to strike. Whenever that happened, they would be ready. He doubted they would have to stay at the cabin for very long before Randall showed himself and was captured.

He walked back into the sheriff's office and Cecile greeted him. With a wig on and from a distance, she would fool anyone. The real Shelby stood beside the door, arms folded and face downturned.

He touched her arms and she looked up at him. "Everything is going to be okay," he assured her. He had to remember that not everyone had his ability to compartmentalize things. He hated leaving her, knowing she was upset, but they couldn't pull this off without him being there. He had to go with Cecile and reminded himself that he was confident in Lawson's ability to protect her if needed.

He leaned in and planted a kiss on Shelby's forehead. "This is going to work," he whispered. "We'll be back soon with this guy in our custody and the answers we're seeking."

She nodded and wrapped her arms around him, then broke the embrace.

Paul climbed into the truck and headed off. He gripped the steering wheel as they drove. Cecile was seated beside him and it was startling to see her in the blond wig and wearing Shelby's clothes.

Paul spotted lights in the rearview mirror and gripped the steering wheel. He sped up as his heart kicked into high gear. Was Randall going to try to ambush them again on the road? He clicked on the mic in his ear, just in case.

Cecile saw his action, then glanced behind them. "What is it?"

"Maybe nothing." But maybe not. He kept a close eye on the car, then breathed a sigh of relief as it turned off and disappeared. "False alarm."

He couldn't allow himself to get worked up over every little thing. Who knew when Randall would take the opportunity to strike? He had to settle his mind that this might be a long night of waiting.

He pulled into the clearing of the cabin and cut the engine. He was comforted to know that he couldn't see Josh and the other deputies despite the light from the cabin. Yet the earbud in his ear told him they were out there, watching and waiting. Everyone was anxious to get this ruse over with and bring this guy down, even though they didn't have nearly the stakes in it that he did. Keeping Shelby safe had become more than a duty to him. It was his mission now. He wouldn't allow anyone to harm her.

He parked and got out and ushered Cecile into the cabin the same way he would have Shelby, in order to keep up the facade. They had no way of knowing whether or not Randall was watching, so they had to keep up the facade and maintain appearances at all times.

He unloaded supplies from the truck, then locked the cabin door and glanced around before hitting the mic on his headset. "We're inside."

"Roger that," Josh responded. "We're all

in position and watching. Will let you know when we see someone approaching."

Cecile sat on the sofa, a small smile playing on her lips.

He looked at her and saw her smirking. "What?"

"I've known you for a long time, Paul. This is the first time I've ever seen you like this."

"Like what?"

"This woman, Shelby, she's important to you, isn't she?"

He didn't respond. Yes, he'd fallen hard for Shelby, but that didn't mean it was something he was all that comfortable discussing. He still couldn't fully grasp the weight of his feelings. He'd never felt anything like it. She'd become so important to him and he couldn't lose her.

But he'd known Cecile a long time and decided to confide in her. "I've fallen in love with her and I don't know what to do."

Cecile looked at him, undoubtedly surprised by his sudden candor. "What is there to do? If you love her, tell her so."

"How can someone like Shelby ever love me, Cecile? I'm a broken, shattered mess. She deserves better than me."

She stood and walked over to him. "You

listen to me, Paul Avery. I've known you for a very long time and you are not broken. You're a good man fighting something beyond your control. Any woman could count herself blessed to fall in love with you—and to have your love in return."

"You don't know what I've seen, Cecile. You don't know the things I've done."

"I don't need to know. I know your heart."

"This guy we're battling, Randall. He's like me. He's probably seen things unimaginable to some people. I could have ended up like him, just a killer for hire."

"No, you couldn't. Maybe you both have the same training and a similar skill set, but he chose to do unspeakable acts in the name of money. He chose to be a bringer of death, while you chose to protect life. That's the difference between you, Paul, and it has nothing to do with what you've seen or what your training is. It's all about your heart. He chose the darkness. You chose the light."

"I don't feel very light filled."

"You could have let Shelby die multiple times, but you didn't. You stepped in to protect her, even at the risk of your own life. You made the decision to do the right thing when it mattered. I don't know this man, but he can't have much of a heart for God, given the things he's done."

"Do you really think God wants anything to do with me?" Just days ago, he would have said words like that with a scoff, certain that the answer was no. But now he was really asking. He truly wanted to know. He wanted to believe again.

She reached for his hand. "Oh Paul, of course He does. He loves you. And I believe Shelby loves you too. Now you have to learn to love yourself."

His earpiece clicked on with the sound of his brother's voice asking everyone for a status update. Deputy Morrison gave the all clear.

Paul clicked on his mic. "Still clear here too." He picked up his rifle and walked to the window, staring out into the night. His soul felt as dark as the sky outside, yet he still saw light reflecting off the moon and shining its glow over the area. Was God's radiance trying to do the same? Trying to push its way through his shadowed soul? He hoped so. He wanted it. He wanted to remember what it was like to feel whole again, to love again. He knew he was already most of the way there. He'd fallen hard for Shelby, and there was no getting around it. Now he just needed to figure out how to deal with it.

Paul spotted something in the woods he was sure was a glint from a scope. He keyed his mic. "Josh, is one of your men in the trees on the south side?"

"No, why?"

"It's him. I see him." He pushed open the door and knelt down to fire just as the sniper began shooting. The guy had managed to sneak in and take up position someplace they hadn't prepared for. But he wasn't going to get away this time.

He took several shots with his rifle as Cecile hollered at him to come back inside and take cover, but he couldn't let this guy follow his usual MO of getting off his rounds, then fleeing. He had to catch up to him. He took off running, his breath heavy and ragged and his leg screaming at him. He disregarded it. Randall fired off several more shots that missed him by inches, but he didn't slow down. He heard yelling in the distance and in his ear.

"Paul, stop!" Josh was hollering. "Stand down."

Paul ignored him, even as several pops of gunfire went off again.

As he reached the tree line, someone grabbed him, pulling him down. Paul raised his gun only to see Josh standing over him. His heart beat a mile a minute and he struggled to catch his breath. "I nearly shot you!"

"What did you think you were doing?"

"Going after the shooter."

"I told you to stand down. This is my operation, and when I tell you to stand down, you'd better stand down."

"I saw him, Josh. He's there in the trees." He glanced up and spotted a dark figure fleeing. "He's getting away."

"He's not going anywhere. I've got Winston and Morrison going after him."

"Let me go. I need to be there." He jumped to his feet and pushed past his brother, who tried to stop him.

"You're hurt, Paul. He's not getting away. The situation's handled. You don't have to be the one to capture him."

"Yes, I do!" Paul spun around to face him. "Don't you get it? It has to be me, Josh. I have to end this. This has to stop now, tonight. I can't let him continue to hurt Shelby."

"As long as he's caught, what difference does it make who does the takedown? Why does it have to be you? Why does that matter so much?"

"Because I love her! I won't let anything else happen to her. I can't lose her." He dropped his gun and pushed his hands through his hair. Sweat was pouring off him, but all he could focus on was capturing this guy and keeping Shelby safe.

There was a beat before Josh replied. When he did, his voice was soft. "I didn't realize she meant so much to you."

He stared in his brother's direction, and a realization hit him hard in the chest. "She means everything to me. I've been walking around in darkness for years, and suddenly, she brought light into my life. For the first time in forever, someone has made me want to be a better person."

Josh stood, then started to speak but stopped when yelling followed by several pops of gunfire filled the air. He pressed his earpiece. "Morrison, what's happening?"

Paul clambered to his feet and waited for several long, heavy moments before the deputy responded. "We've got him, sheriff. The shooter is in custody."

The relief that flowed through Paul at those words was so overwhelming that he nearly doubled over in gratitude. Randall was in cuffs. That meant Shelby was safe for now.

His brother broke into a smile and he grabbed Paul's shoulder and pulled him into a quick hug before he urged him forward. "Let's go take this guy back to the station and process him. Then you and your lady need to have a long conversation."

Paul hurried as best he could along with Josh as relief and gratitude filled him. This nightmare was nearly over .

Shelby watched as the men hauled their captive into the back of a cruiser. The scene that had unfolded from the video feeds on the cameras mounted on their chests had been unbelievable, and she couldn't stop recalling the words Paul had shouted to his brother. Clearly, he hadn't realized she could hear his every word.

He loved her. Those words had knocked her off her feet for several minutes. She'd been unable to breathe or comprehend anything except the knowledge that Paul Avery was in love with her.

Tears slid down her cheeks, and she wiped them away. Hearing his confession of love had done a number on her. It was everything she'd hardly even allowed herself to dream of. She'd never imagined that she could possibly feel this much for another person. She'd made a promise to herself after her brother died that she wouldn't ever love someone again, but she'd broken that vow with Paul. She loved him. And after hearing the passion in his voice for her, she loved him all the more.

But she also couldn't deny the risks he'd taken tonight in the name of keeping her safe. He'd acted reckless and impulsively and could have just as easily been killed as taken Randall down. Even when Josh had ordered him to stop, he hadn't listened. That reminded her that all she'd ever wanted could be taken away at a moment's notice by one hasty act. And Paul was nothing if not unpredictable. He would step into danger to protect her and others without a second thought for his own safety.

She pressed her hand to her mouth as she realized the truth—loving Paul Avery would eventually leave her heartbroken.

She glanced up as cheers from the bullpen alerted her that the group had returned. As the other deputies congratulated the victors on their win, Shelby peered through the glass and spotted Josh and Lawson leading a handcuffed Jason Randall through the bull-pen and back to the cells. Paul followed behind them, his rifle still at the ready in case there was trouble.

Her heart swelled. She'd never been prouder of him than at this moment, when she could tell that the burden she'd seen him shouldering was gone. He had a right to be proud. He and his brothers had captured Randall. He'd made certain she was safe. Tears slid down her face because she knew the truth. She owed this man her life. So many times over.

But she could never give him her heart.

He pushed open the conference room door and stepped inside. His face lit up in a smile as soon as he saw her. Her resolve faded when he pulled her into his arms and kissed her. She could live in those arms forever and she wanted to, but...

She broke away from him and put some space between them. She had to keep her distance if she was going to get through this. She wanted to be with this man more than she'd ever wanted anything, but loving him was only going to end in heartbreak for her. She just couldn't take that, not again. She'd already lost her brother. She wouldn't be able to stand losing Paul too. Better to let him go now, before their connection became too great.

But even as she thought it, she knew it was already too late to walk away with her heart intact. She'd fallen hard for this navy SEAL. Getting over him would be difficult, but it certainly was better than burying another person she loved.

"We did it, Shelby. We got Randall." His face practically sparkled with glee.

"I know. I watched it happen from here." She motioned toward the monitor.

"Then you saw it went smoothly."

She nodded instead of answering him, and he cocked his head, observing her. "Something is wrong. What's bothering you?"

Her first instinct was to shut down and push him away, but she owed it to him to be truthful, to give him the full explanation. It wasn't his fault, but he had to know why she was doing this. She wanted him to understand. "I'm going back to Dallas." She hadn't planned to say that, but as soon as the words came out, she knew this plan was for the best. It was time to get out of this town and head back to her life. "Now that you have Randall in custody, I assume it's safe?"

He gave her a look mixed with apprehension and confusion. "You're not in danger from Randall anymore, but there is still the matter of David."

"I can handle David."

"Really? Because he hired someone to kill you."

"Only because he didn't have the guts to do it himself. Once he realizes his plan failed, he won't be hiring anyone else." She was more convinced of that than ever. David was a coward and always had been.

"Well, just in case, I'll be contacting the Dallas PD to pick him up. Once we have a confession from Randall, he'll do jail time for this."

He reached for her again and she moved away from him. When he spoke, his voice held confusion and uncertainty. The smile he'd been wearing as he walked Randall into the station faded. "What's going on, Shelby?"

"I don't want to hurt you, Paul, but what's been happening between us can't go any further. It needs to end. Now."

His eyes searched hers looking for some reason behind her unexpected decision. "Is this for…ethical reasons?" he asked. "If it's about the evaluation, I don't care about that any longer. I'll find someone else. If that means staying off the team for a while longer, I will. You're more important to me than that."

She shook her head. "No, it's more than that. It's us. I can't be with you, Paul. I watched you on that video. I saw the risks you took."

"Risks to save your life. I would do anything to keep you safe, Shelby. Anything."

"I know that and I do appreciate it, but this went beyond that. The deputies were handling it, and you still ran into danger. You didn't even listen to Josh when he told you to stand down. I can't fall in love with someone who takes such risks. When my brother died, it nearly destroyed me. I couldn't stand losing you, too, Paul. I just couldn't."

"You're not going to lose me, Shelby."

"Really? Can you promise me that? Can you promise that you'll never go into another dangerous mission? That you'll never infiltrate a terrorist compound or parachute behind enemy lines to rescue hostages?"

"This is about me being a SEAL? Are you asking me to give it up?"

For a moment, hopefulness bloomed. Would that fix this? Could she be with him if he left military service? Then the hope faded again as she realized the truth. "It wouldn't matter, Paul. You are a SEAL. It's in your nature. Even if you never return to your team, you still have those tendencies to jump into dangerous situations without thinking of the consequences. Like you did tonight with Randall."

"What are you talking about?"

"I saw you, Paul. You ran at Randall as if he didn't have a gun pointed right at you. Even your brother thought you acted recklessly."

"I did that to keep you safe, Shelby. Don't you know there is nothing I wouldn't do for you?"

She turned away from him before she lost her resolve and because she couldn't stand the pain written across his expression.

He stood behind her, so close she nearly fell back into his arms. He rested his hands on her shoulders, holding her gently. "Don't do this, Shelby. You're afraid. I realize that, but don't throw away what we have because of fear. Fight it. Fight for us."

She turned and stared up into his hopeful face. She wanted to crawl right into his arms, but she couldn't. Tears slipped from her eyes. "I don't think I can."

"Shelby, I love you. No one could ever love you as much as I do." He dropped his hands from her shoulders, pulled off his cap and wrung it in his hands as he paced in front of her, clearly trying to work out some way to change her mind. "Do you love me?" he asked abruptly.

She had to bite her lip to keep the words from tumbling out. Yes, she loved him, but she couldn't give in to that feeling. She pulled all of her willpower together and looked up into his eyes. "I don't."

"You're lying."

Of course she was lying! "I could never be happy with you if I'll always be waiting for the other shoe to drop. And it will, Paul. If we stay together, one day, I'll get that call that you've done something that's gotten you killed."

"So you're pushing me away because you don't want to lose me? That doesn't make a lick of sense."

She knew it didn't, but the problem was so much bigger than that. "Tell me, how could I ever fully commit to you, knowing that our future could end in your dying."

"Everyone dies, Shelby."

She shook her head, her resolve firm. "Not

everybody runs toward death, headfirst. I'm sorry. I don't want to hurt you, but I just can't do this."

He looked at her, then apparently gave up trying to change her mind. He turned and opened the conference room door but stopped to look back at her before he walked out. "I can't believe you're really ending this."

She couldn't believe it, either, but she had no choice. She would never survive if she allowed this to continue and then lost him.

She stared through the glass and watched Paul disappear through a door in the back. She turned around and spotted several people in the office averting their eyes. They'd obviously overheard their conversation and were trying not to make it obvious.

Shelby pulled the blinds closed, then fell onto a chair and cried. She sobbed into her hands as her heart broke. She still believed it was the right decision, but that didn't mean it hadn't been a difficult one to make.

When her tears were spent, a new emotion pushed its way to the front.

Anger.

David had caused all of this with his greed and cowardice. He'd pushed her into Paul's life, then created a need for Paul to protect her. Suddenly, her blood boiled at how David had manipulated her. He'd used her for her work, then taken shortcuts behind her back, deceiving everyone, raking in money illegally and immorally and trying to find the easy way out once he'd been discovered.

She couldn't wait to confront him. She needed him to know that he hadn't won, that he'd hurt her, but he hadn't broken her. She would pick up the pieces of the life he'd shattered, and he would go to jail for his crimes. He hadn't won. It was suddenly very important to her that he knew he hadn't won.

She decided on the spot to drive to Dallas right away to confront him. She would never get to sleep tonight, not knowing this heavy burden was weighing her down. If she didn't confront him before the Dallas PD arrived to arrest him, she might never get the opportunity to tell him off, face-to-face.

She found Bree in the breakroom and asked to borrow her car. Bree handed over the key but looked surprised by the request. Shelby walked outside and got into her vehicle, then turned it toward Dallas. It was time to end this.

TEN

Paul showered in the locker room, then changed into clean clothes. He didn't go back to the conference space, where Shelby was. He couldn't look at her right now and be reminded of how she was throwing away their future out of fear. Instead, he headed for the interview room, where deputies had moved Randall for questioning after the booking process. Paul glanced at him through the viewing window. The man was cuffed to the table and Deputy Winston was standing guard inside.

The SEAL tattoos confirmed Paul's suspicions that they were dealing with someone with special training, but he still couldn't believe anyone who had vowed to protect and serve his country could turn to murder for hire. It sickened him, degrading the very vow that each service member took.

Josh rounded the corner with a file in his

hand. "We ran his prints and got a hit from the military database. His real name is Jason Roundtree. He's a navy SEAL who served six tours overseas and just recently returned from medical leave. He was shot during a hostage rescue, leaving him with a bad knee that hasn't properly healed."

Paul glanced at the file. The bad knee explained why he'd been slow to leave his sniper's nest and why he'd left his rifle behind at the ranch.

"You want to sit in on the questioning?"

Paul nodded and followed his brother as he opened the door and walked into the interview room. He took one chair on the opposite side of the table from Roundtree, and Paul pulled out the other one.

Josh opened the file. He was calm and collected the way Paul knew he should be. Paul was doing his best to appear so on the outside, but on the inside, every instinct in his body was screaming to hop over this table and demand answers from this rogue operative. The man who had demeaned everything Paul held dear. He'd tarnished the SEAL reputation and tried to murder the woman Paul cared for deeply, despite everything.

"We know who you are," Josh said, pulling out his military sheet and showing it to him.

Roundtree shrugged. "So?"

"So why would a decorated navy SEAL want to kill Shelby Warren? What has she ever done to you?"

Roundtree leaned back in his seat, his face expressionless, a tactic no doubt learned during his training. They were taught never to give anything away. And this was nothing but a simple interview by a small-town sheriff's office. Roundtree could probably hold out for much longer than Josh or him.

"Just because you're not deployed doesn't mean you don't still owe a duty to your country. I'll tell you what I believe. I believe this was merely a job for you. Now, that's bad enough—but we want to put away the real perpetrator. The person who hired you. As long as he's free, Shelby remains in danger." He pulled out David's photograph and pushed it across the table.

Roundtree stared at it. "Why are you showing me a picture of Dr. Sloan?"

"Because he's the one who hired you to kill Shelby," Josh replied readily—but Paul knew his brother well enough to hear the edge of confusion in his voice. This wasn't the reaction he'd been expecting.

Roundtree pushed the photo away. "You don't know anything. Dr. Sloan didn't hire me."

Now he'd caught Paul's attention. He leaned forward. "Then who did?" When the man didn't answer, Paul slammed his fist down on the table. "Who hired you? If it wasn't David, then who?"

Roundtree leaned back in his seat, a smug smile forming on his face. "Sounds like I've got something you need. Maybe we can make a deal."

"You've shot three of my deputies," Josh reminded him. "There won't be any deals for you. Now, either you tell us your employer or you go down for this all by yourself."

Roundtree looked from Josh to Paul and back again before heaving a loud sigh. "Colette Sanders. She's the one who hired me."

Stunned shock rocked Paul back into his seat. "Colette? The receptionist?"

"Yes, the receptionist. I don't know if she was working for anyone else, but she was the one who handled the details. Let me tell you, that woman is scary—and absolutely ruthless."

"Why don't you tell us what happened," Josh said, pressing on Paul's arm to sit down.

"I was seeing Dr. Sloan for a while for some trouble I've been having sleeping. He gave me these pills and they helped for a time. When they stopped working, he prescribed something else. It didn't take long for me to grow dependent on them."

"You got addicted?" Just like Bobby Goldman from the rehab center.

"Yeah, that's right. So the doctor recommended I go to this rehab facility run by his friend. Everything was fine until Colette called me and told me she wanted me to kill a woman. I said no way. Then she said she was going to tell my commanding officer about my drug problems and how I've been in rehab."

"He didn't know?"

Roundtree shook his head and leaned back in his chair. "No. I paid the doc under the table to keep it out of my official medical records."

"Why would Colette want Shelby dead?"

"I don't know. She said something about how Dr. Warren was going to shut everything down. That's all I know. She said if I didn't do this, we would all end up going to jail and I would lose my career. I would be kicked off the teams." He shook his head. "I couldn't risk that. Besides, I figured taking this job would help hone my skills. They'd gotten rusty since I've been off duty."

"Hone your skills?" Paul repeated, suddenly furious. "That's what you call taking a job to kill a woman?"

He ignored Paul's outrage. "If I'd been sharper, you never would have managed to sneak up on me at the ranch and I wouldn't have had to leave my rifle."

"And the first shot at Shelby's office? What happened that day? You were so slow I managed to catch up to you then too."

He shrugged and rubbed his leg. "Bad knee. It catches sometimes. I can't always get to my feet as fast as I used to."

Paul was disgusted by this man's attitude. He showed no regret over agreeing to kill an innocent woman—the only part he had a problem with was that he hadn't been physically capable of killing her as efficiently as he'd hoped.

Paul understood being caught up in something, and even going to see a doctor off the books to keep his medical records clean, but when did being a SEAL become more important than a person's life? A person's integrity?

"I have to tell her about Colette," Paul said.

Josh nodded and Paul got up and left, then headed down to the conference room. He pushed open the door and saw only Bree inside. "Do you know where Shelby is?"

"She asked to borrow my car, so I let her. She left a half hour ago."

He grunted in irritation. It was bad enough she was pushing him away, now she was going off on her own? Of course, with Roundtree out of play, she probably thought it was fine for her to leave without protection, but why hadn't she told him where she was headed?

"Did she say where she was going?"

"No, she didn't say, and I didn't ask."

He slipped his phone from his pocket, then realized they'd never replaced hers after it was damaged in the attack at the hotel.

Bree must have seen him hesitate. "I think my cell is in the car. You might be able to reach her that way."

He entered the number, but it went straight to voice mail. The device must be turned off or on silent. She probably didn't even realize it was there. Just in case, he tried again then sent a text message asking her to call him immediately.

He slid his cell back into his pocket, praying she would get the message and would respond soon, but as he headed back to the interview room, he remembered her saying she was going back to Dallas. He paused. Surely, she hadn't meant tonight. But what if she had? She had every reason to believe that David was the one behind the attacks against her and confronting him would be dangerous enough, but she didn't know the truth. She didn't know to watch out for Colette or whomever the receptionist was working for.

Shelby was still in danger as long as this woman was still out there.

Shelby turned into the parking lot at her office complex, parked and cut the engine. David's car was sitting outside, but the building looked dark and foreboding.

The entrance was unlocked. She stepped inside and headed down the long hallway toward David's office. A sliver of light shone from beneath his door to let her know he was indeed there.

She pushed it open and found him slumped across his desk, his heavy breathing indicating that he was asleep. But as she approached him, he jerked up, suddenly awake. His eyes grew wide with surprise. "Shelby! You startled me. What are you doing here?"

"I'd guess you're surprised to see me, aren't you?"

"I am. Very surprised."

He sounded so natural, so normal, that she felt her anger spike. "How could you do it, David?"

"What have I done now?"

"You hired a man to kill me."

He jumped to his feet, mouth open in shock. "I did not! Shelby, I don't know what you're talking about."

"Don't play games with me, David. I know he was your patient. I remember seeing him here before." That was the vague recollection she'd been trying to place.

"I don't know who you think you saw, but I didn't hire anyone to try to kill you. Why would I want to do that?"

"You tell me. What did I ever do to you, David? I thought we worked well together."

"Shelby, listen to me. I did not hire anyone to kill you." He moved around the desk and grabbed her arms and suddenly she realized the foolishness of coming here. Yes, he was a coward, but he'd hired someone to murder her to protect himself. If he was feeling backed into a corner, he might find the strength to kill her himself now that she was within his grasp and knew his deeds had been discovered.

She pulled away and put some space between them. "Then how do you explain the man who shot at me here and has followed me to Courtland County and has tried to kill me multiple times? How could he have known where I'd be?"

"I can't explain it. I don't know."

"Then tell me how, when I told you I was going to that cabin to hide out, that he knew to attack me there? You were the only one I told."

"You were attacked at the cabin? But I..." He shook his head, struggling to answer. "I don't know, but I promise you it wasn't me. I didn't send him after you. I've never tried to harm you. Why would I even consider that, Shelby?"

"Because of Bobby Goldman and Adam Sheffield and how many other countless patients whose evaluations you forged—with my signature—after you accepted bribes to change the recommendation. You altered my forms, David, which is fraud, and you knew you were going to jail once the truth came out."

His face paled as he stared at her, then he

returned to the other side of his desk where he fell into his chair. "I did do those things. I admit that."

Finally, they were getting somewhere. "And you knew that I'd discovered what you were doing and planned to turn you in."

"No. When you confronted me about Michael Finley, I thought for certain you were on to what I was doing, but you seemed to accept my explanation. I hoped it was over. I'm not proud of myself."

"You'll lose your license for this."

"Maybe, but that doesn't mean I sent this man to kill you."

She saw the resignation in his face at his misdeeds and the weariness in his expression—and realized that she believed him. He hadn't hired Randall to come after her. But if it hadn't been David, then who had employed Randall?

"I'm sorry I accused you," she told David. "I owe you an apology."

He gave her a wry half smile. "I'm not exactly innocent, but I promise you, I would never try to hurt you."

"But you *did* hurt these men who came to you. How many did you let slip through, David?"

"More than I'd like to admit. A lot of them became addicted to the pills I prescribed, hoping medication could see them through. It got to be a real problem. My friend Caleb runs the rehab center and I've been giving him a lot of business lately."

"You've been sending your patients to the rehab center and taking a kickback."

He rubbed his face and didn't answer. He didn't need to. His corruption seemed never ending. But he'd made those choices and he would be the one to suffer the consequences for them. They were horrible and he deserved to be held accountable—but he wasn't guilty of conspiracy to commit murder. There was some relief in that.

As her anger dissipated, she fell onto a chair and sighed. She'd been foolish for acting on her anger and coming here alone. She'd blamed David for something he hadn't done and she still didn't even know who it was who wanted her dead.

She'd made a mess of everything. She'd acted recklessly, just as she'd accused Paul of doing. She'd made the choice to come here, just as Randall had made the decision to target her, just as David had made the decision to choose money over his ethics…and just as her brother had chosen to walk back into active duty rather than dealing with his problems.

She ran a hand through her hair. She'd been holding on for so long to this anger and resentment over her brother's death, and she was weary of it. She was ready to let it go. It wasn't God's fault that Steven had died, any more than it was His fault that she'd acted rashly and pushed Paul away. Free will meant that everyone had the right to make their own choices—even if they were the wrong ones.

She only hoped she hadn't ruined her opportunity at happiness forever.

She bit back tears recalling the pain in Paul's expression as he'd declared his love for her. He'd been right about her allowing fear to dictate her path. She needed to apologize, beg his forgiveness and pray it wasn't too late.

"I need to borrow your phone." She reached for the one on his desk, unwilling to risk another moment passing without Paul knowing the truth—that she loved him and wanted to spend the rest of her life with him.

Suddenly, she heard something behind her. She turned to see Colette standing in the doorway, a gun in her hand pointed right at Shelby. "I'd hold off on that call if I were you, Dr. Warren."

"Colette, what are you doing?"

The young woman's stance was firm and her face twisted. "What that idiot couldn't. I'm taking care of you."

David leaped to his feet. "Colette, what have you done?"

"What I had to do. I couldn't risk the setup we have with Caleb."

"*We* have?" Shelby asked. She turned to David. "You've got Colette dragged into this too?"

"No one had to drag me into anything. I'm a single mom, remember? I needed the money I received from both David and Caleb to keep my mouth shut about their tricks to play the system. I overheard that conversation you had with David about changing the recommendation on Michael Finley. Then when you decided to start looking through your files for other instances, I knew you were going to find out the truth about what was happening. He said you were going to compromise our entire operation. I couldn't allow that."

Shelby was stunned. This entire office was corrupt. "You're the one who sent Randall to kill me?"

She smirked. "His name isn't Randall. It's Jason Roundtree. I knew the truth about his drug dependence and threatened to tell his commander unless he took care of you. He balked at first, but his career was on the line, so he took the deal. When I heard Roundtree had been arrested, I knew I had to take care of you myself. I bugged David's office so I knew you were here."

Shelby's mind was racing with the unbelievable truth of it all. Colette was the mastermind behind the attacks on her? It didn't make any sense. How had this been happening and she'd never realized it?

But Shelby wasn't going to stand here and be a victim in her own office. She wasn't going to allow Colette to take her down to hide their misdeeds. She lunged at Colette while the other woman's attention was centered on David. Shelby reached for the gun and tried to pull it away from her, but Colette screamed at her and fought back, refusing to release it without a fight.

Colette yanked at the weapon hard and a shot went off, sending both women tumbling backward. Shelby jumped up to see what had happened. David gave a small cry and she turned to him. A pool of red was blossoming on his shirt where the bullet had hit him. He reached for the desk to keep from falling, but it did no good. He collapsed onto the floor.

Shelby turned to Colette, whose eyes were wide with surprise. "You shot him."

"I—I didn't mean to shoot him."

No, she'd meant to shoot Shelby.

The shock in Colette's face turned to contempt, and she scrambled to her feet and grabbed for the gun, now lying on the floor. Shelby dived for it too. She couldn't allow Colette to reach it first. Colette had already shot David and attempted to kill Shelby by proxy. She had everything to lose unless Shelby died. Only then could she hope to get away with it all.

Oh God, please don't let this be the end. I want to live. I want to tell Paul how much I love him. Please help me!

Sounds in the hallway told her someone was coming.

"Shelby!"

Paul's voice flowed over her like a balm, and tears filled her eyes. He'd come after her. It wasn't too late for her to tell him how much she loved him.

"I'm here," she called, but that moment, when her attention was divided between

Paul's voice and the struggle, Colette took full advantage of it.

She shoved Shelby, sending her stumbling. She caught her footing and turned just in time to see Colette raise the weapon and fire.

A blinding white-hot pain ripped through her. She glanced down at her hand on her stomach and saw it was wet with blood. Colette had shot her.

Paul's heart stopped when he heard the gunshot. He barreled down the hallway and burst into the office just as Shelby grabbed her stomach. When she moved her hand, it was bloody.

He ran to her, catching her in his arms as her legs gave out and she fell. From the corner of his eye, he saw Josh snatch the gun from Colette and put her in handcuffs, but his attention was mostly focused on the woman in his arms. Her face was growing pale and she was limp in his arms.

"Stay with me, Shelby," he urged her. His heart was in full-panic mode. He couldn't compartmentalize this. Fear rushed through him and he couldn't think of anything to do but beg her not to leave him—and pray.

Josh dialed 9-1-1 on the desk phone then

rushed to check on David before hurrying back to kneel on the floor beside Paul. "David's dead." He pushed Shelby's hands from her stomach and assessed the wound. "We need to slow down this blood loss." He grabbed a jacket from the back of a chair and pressed it against her stomach. "Ambulance is on its way."

She was still losing blood fast. Paul wasn't ready to let her go yet. He tapped her cheek to keep her conscious. "Stay with me, Shelby. Help is on the way."

Her eyes found his and she managed to give him a smile. She reached up her hand and touched his cheek. "I'm sorry, Paul."

He shook his head but pressed his hand over hers. "You have nothing to be sorry about."

"Yes, I do. I said I didn't love you. That was a lie."

His heart soared at hearing her say that, but it sank again when he realized she was fading fast. He turned to his brother. "Where's that ambulance?"

"It'll be here."

He looked back down at Shelby as she struggled to speak against the pain that must be ripping through her. "I—I…"

"You don't have to talk, Shelby. Save your strength." She was going to need it to survive this.

"I do love you," she managed to whisper as a tear slipped from one of her eyes.

He nearly choked on the lump in his throat as he gently wiped it away. "And I love you. Always and forever."

"I didn't want to go without you knowing that."

The sound of sirens in the distance gave him hope. She was going to make it. "No need to worry about that because you're not going anywhere. The ambulance is here. You're staying right here with me for all time."

"I want to," she whispered, sending his heart into a tailspin. She wanted to be with him. She wanted to spend her life with him. Being with her was everything he'd never known he wanted, but now it was the only thing that mattered to him. He wanted nothing else but her at that moment and was ready to give up everything for another opportunity to be with her.

But as her eyelids lowered and she went limp in his arms, he saw his hope for a happy ending fading away with her.

* * *

He'd seen worse wounds but not from someone he cared so much about.

The ambulance had finally arrived and taken Shelby to the hospital. Hours of surgery later, he'd been assured that she would live.

But he still had trouble believing it as he watched her lying unconscious.

He held her hand and soaked up the warmth of her, thankful that he and Josh had been in time to call for an ambulance before Colette's bullet had done too much damage. But he hadn't arrived soon enough to prevent the shooting altogether, and that was something he had to live with, something he prayed Shelby could forgive him for.

He thought she would. Her final words to him before she'd passed out had him bursting with happiness. She loved him, and this time he wouldn't let her push him away.

He kissed her hand and felt her move on the bed. He glanced up and saw her studying him.

"How long have you been awake?"

A smile formed on her lips. Lips that were finally starting to get their color back. "I've been watching you for a while." Her voice was hoarse from dehydration and she had to be exhausted, but she tried to sit up.

"Take it easy, Shelby. You just got out of surgery a few hours ago."

"What happened? Colette?"

"Josh and I arrived just after she shot you. She's been booked by Dallas PD. She'll face charges for David's murder in addition to shooting you. And there's also the charge of conspiring with Roundtree to kill you."

She took a deep breath and closed her eyes for a moment, and he thought she was dealing with the pain of knowing David was dead.

"It's over, Shelby. No one else is coming after you. You're safe now." That knowledge should have made them both happy, but now they had to deal with the fallout. He saw everything she'd been through all twisting and turning around in her expression, even before she spoke.

She opened her eyes. "I've lost everything, Paul. My practice, my livelihood, my military contract. It's all gone. I don't know what I'm going to do."

He reached out and stroked her cheek. "Whatever it is, you don't have to figure it out alone. I happen to know someplace where you're very much wanted."

Lighting with anticipation, her eyes searched his. "You still want me?"

"I never stopped wanting you, Shelby. I love you. You're right that everything is different now. I don't know what our futures hold, but I know, whatever it is, we'll face it together. I want to marry you, Shelby. I want to build a life with you and make a family with you. If you'll have me."

Tears shone in her eyes as she nodded her acceptance. "I will. And I promise you this, Paul—I will never leave you again."

He leaned in and kissed her, then stared into the eyes of the woman who made his life complete. "I'll hold you to that promise."

EPILOGUE

Shelby sat in the rocker on the front porch of the Silver Star. Her cat, Ruby, lounged on the porch railing. The poor feline wasn't thrilled with the number of dogs who shared her new environment, but she'd finally gotten used to them.

A pickup hauling a horse trailer came down the lane and stopped in front of the barn. Paul and Lawson climbed out, and Shelby walked off the porch to join them. Paul pulled her into a hug, then motioned toward the mare Lawson led from the trailer. "What do you think?"

"She's beautiful."

After deciding his time with the SEALs was over, Paul had taken a job with Josh, working for the sheriff's office, training deputies in operational tactics. So far, several other jurisdictions had also contacted him to be included in his training. As for Shelby's career path…this mare represented their first step in a new joint venture of starting a horse therapy center for veterans with PTSD.

Even months after being shot, Shelby was taking it easy physically, but her life was not lacking. In fact, God had blessed her in more ways than she'd ever thought possible. She'd gained a husband in Paul, a family in the Averys and a new purpose in her life. It was more than she'd ever expected and she was still in awe of how happy she could be. She'd lost so much, but God had given her so much more.

Paul's hand moved to her stomach and the growing life inside, and he leaned down to kiss her.

The blessings just kept on coming.

* * * * *

*If you enjoyed this Cowboy Lawmen story,
don't miss the previous books in this series
from Virginia Vaughan:*

Texas Twin Abduction
Texas Holiday Hideout

*Available now from
Love Inspired Suspense!*

Dear Reader,

Whenever I put together a synopsis for my editor, it generally includes the phrase "romance was not in her plans" or some variation of that. How often do we make plans for our lives only to have something or someone mess it all up? It happens to me all the time. I make plans to grill outside, then it rains. I make plans to take a trip, then my car breaks down. I make plans to write a book…then Covid-19 hits, the schools shut down and the kids are suddenly and unexpectedly home with me all day. That put a big dent in my writing time! Eventually, we figured out a routine that worked and actually enjoyed the time spent together during the quarantine, but this global pandemic has been a strong reminder to me that I am often not in control of many of the circumstances of my own life. Thankfully, we serve an all-knowing, all-seeing God for whom this global pandemic was no surprise. He had already factored Covid-19 into His plans for my life and yours!

Perhaps that's why this book featured a hero and heroine determined to do their own thing instead of surrendering to the will of

God. In *Texas Target Standoff*, my main characters are each trying to keep a firm grip on what they want to get out of life. Paul, a navy SEAL, wants to return to his team and he's fighting tooth and nail to do so. Shelby is fighting to help people in the only way she knows how, by performing PTSD evaluations for the military. Yet neither of them is making progress toward their goals due to circumstances beyond their control. As we all do, they soon discover that God's plans are always so much better than anything we could imagine.

Thank you for joining me for Paul and Shelby's story. I am excitedly looking forward to little sister Kellyanne's story in the next book.

I love to hear from my readers! You can contact me online at my website www.virginiavaughanonline.com or on my Facebook page at www.facebook.com/ginvaughanbooks.

Virginia

Get 4 FREE REWARDS!

We'll send you 2 FREE Books plus 2 FREE Mystery Gifts.

Love Inspired books feature uplifting stories where faith helps guide you through life's challenges and discover the promise of a new beginning.

FREE
Value Over
$20

Get 4 FREE REWARDS!

We'll send you 2 FREE Books plus 2 FREE Mystery Gifts.

Harlequin Heartwarming Larger-Print books will connect you to uplifting stories where the bonds of friendship, family and community unite.

Her Hometown Detective
Elizabeth Mowers

Bride on the Run
Anna J. Stewart

FREE
Value Over
$20

YES! Please send me 2 FREE Harlequin Heartwarming Larger-Print novels and my 2 FREE mystery gifts (gifts worth about $10 retail). After receiving them, if I don't wish to receive any more books, I can return the shipping statement marked "cancel." If I don't cancel, I will receive 4 brand-new larger-print novels every month and be billed just $5.74 per book in the U.S. or $6.24 per book in Canada. That's a savings of at least 21% off the cover price. It's quite a bargain! Shipping and handling is just 50¢ per book in the U.S. and $1.25 per book in Canada.* I understand that accepting the 2 free books and gifts places me under no obligation to buy anything. I can always return a shipment and cancel at any time. The free books and gifts are mine to keep no matter what I decide.

161/361 HDN GNPZ

Name (please print)

Address   Apt. #

City   State/Province   Zip/Postal Code

Email: Please check this box ☐ if you would like to receive newsletters and promotional emails from Harlequin Enterprises ULC and its affiliates. You can unsubscribe anytime.

Mail to the **Harlequin Reader Service:**
IN U.S.A.: P.O. Box 1341, Buffalo, NY 14240-8531
IN CANADA: P.O. Box 603, Fort Erie, Ontario L2A 5X3

Want to try 2 free books from another series? Call 1-800-873-8635 or visit www.ReaderService.com.

HARLEQUIN SELECTS COLLECTION

19 FREE BOOKS IN ALL!

From Robyn Carr to RaeAnne Thayne to Linda Lael Miller and Sherryl Woods we promise (actually, GUARANTEE!) each author in the Harlequin Selects collection has seen their name on the *New York Times* or *USA TODAY* bestseller lists!